FLOATER

Lucius Shepard

Introduction by Jeffrey Ford

PS Publishing 2003

FIRST EDITION

Floater
Copyright © 2003 by Lucius Shepard

Introduction
Copyright © 2003 by Jeffrey Ford

Cover
Copyright © 2003 by Edward Miller

Published in September 2003 by PS Publishing LLP
by arrangement with the author.
All rights reserved by the author.

ISBN
1 902880 79 X (Paperback)
1 902880 80 3 (Hardcover)

PS Publishing LLP
Hamilton House
4 Park Avenue
Harrogate HG2 9BQ
ENGLAND

e-mail
crowth1@attglobal.net

Internet
http://www.pspublishing.co.uk

Floater

by Lucius Shepard

[signature]

Lucius Shepard

Introduction

By Jeffrey Ford

I first became conscious of the writing of Lucius Shepard
through a handful of essays of his that appeared on *Event
Horizon*, an early webzine edited by Ellen Datlow and Rob
Killheffer. One of the pieces, "The Littleton Follies," was about
the student killings at Columbine, and the thing that marked it in
my memory was the writer's ability to step back and see this
tragedy in the larger context of the hypocritical society that in
some ways had fostered it. Also very evident was a hilarious,
cutting sense of humor that at no time struck me as irreverent
(given the grievous nature of the event in question), but instead
served to illuminate the absurdity of those political pundits who
used the brutal high school attack for their own ends. When I
came across the following lines, concerning William Bennett's co-
opting the shootings to make hay for the reactionary right's
"family values/America in moral decline" argument, they caused
me to laugh aloud as hard as I ever had at any piece of prose in
my reading life:

> But this particular version of the old standard has been
> made especially nauseating in my view thanks to the
> gloomy, rhinoceros-like presence of William Bennett,
> the nation's self-appointed moral policeman, a man who
> delights in referring to his days of public service when
> he was—as he likes to call himself—"drug czar." (And
> what a bang-up job he did in solving that moral crisis,

huh, folks?) Bennett, who has discovered that one can make a nice living by being a professional prude, often delivers his neo-Puritan cant with a lugubrious spite that has caused me to wonder at times if this blue-serge-suited tub of goo isn't really Sheriff Andy's Aunt Bea made up to play Cotton Mather in Mayberry's annual Segregation Day Festival.

After I calmed down and wiped the tears out of my eyes, I went in search of Shepard, trying to find whatever else he had written. I discovered a few very good novels (especially *The Golden*, a tripped-out vampire novel the likes of which, I guarantee, you have not yet seen) and a treasure trove of some of the finest stories in the contemporary speculative fiction genre—"Crocodile Rock," "Radiant Green Star," "Eternity and Afterward," "The Jaguar Hunter," "Beast of the Heartland," etc.

Although he is a versatile writer who can do it all well, there are certain aspects of Shepard's writing that allow him to be at his very best at the novella length. The most obvious of these is the fact that his fictions are centered on his characters. Their interactions, their development, their catharsis, are precisely where the story germinates and gains its impetus. The novella format allows his protagonists and their supporting casts time to breathe and reach a convincing weight. In this sense his long stories are much like novels. On the other hand, there is a constant progression and economy at hand that reminds one of the best short stories. You will rarely find a scene that, although it might reveal some facet of character, does not advance the storyline as well. There are few if any long meditative passages for their own sake, the likes of which one might find in a novel. Shepard is able to work this special alchemy because his prose is a careful balance of evocative imagery and concision. In other words, one gets the most bang for one's reading buck in each scene. The focus of a given paragraph might be the setting, but then the setting is a reflection of the character's present psychology, which in turn is analogous to a given aspect of the theme of the story. And all the time, the plot is moving inexorably forward.

Shepard is one of those very few fiction writers whose craft has developed to the point where he can succinctly capture in words anything his imagination can conceive. The real beauty of this, though, is that most readers would be unaware, save on a subconscious level, of these effects, which is, of course, the way it should be. The result is that his novellas are like a science fictional phenomenon, themselves: although from the outside they have a definite physical limit derived from plot and pacing, they are hugely expansive within those limits.

I have seen Shepard's fiction likened to that of Joseph Conrad, and this makes perfect sense as far as the settings and themes of the stories go—personal dramas played out in exotic locales, the Third World, expatriation, adventure, the clash of cultures. Conrad also utilized strong, energetic plots as magnets with which to ground his philosophical concerns, but let's face it, old Joe's prose was as thick as molasses. Shepard's writing style is more reminiscent, as far as I am concerned, of that of another author who had seen much of the world hidden from Western eyes, namely Robert Louis Stevenson. With both Shepard and Stevenson, the writing, though succinctly detailed enough to be vivid, flows like water, a perfect variation of both long and short sentences that emulates the musical rise and fall of a natural storyteller's voice.

Shepard's use of the "genre" of the fantastic is also quite interesting, for many of his stories begin in settings easily recognizable as locales in the real world. There is a startling and often stark realism to the pieces at their outset. Only slowly, a grain at a time, does the supernatural begin to slip into the plot, so that the reader often starts out on solid ground and, while getting caught up in the characters' personal dilemmas, hardly notices that the strange is rising until they are knee-deep in it. This graceful, gradual incursion of the weird, only possible at novella length, builds suspense and makes the fantastic readily believable when it finally attains its full-blown form.

All of the various techniques I have catalogued above are at play in the new novella, *Floater*, you hold in your hands. I believe it will be considered one of Shepard's best. It is obviously based on the Amadou Diallo shooting that took place in New York a couple of years ago, wherein three New York City detectives emptied their guns into an innocent Haitian immigrant as he reached for his wallet to get his ID. The incident and the subsequent investigation were fishy as hell, capping a protracted series of incidents of police abuse in the city and further fueling tensions between minority communities and law enforcement.

Shepard's story adds voodoo to the mix of just such an incident. At a brief glance one might think that having the victim be a practitioner of voodoo is an attempt to exonerate the detectives, but that is only if one assumes voodoo to be a negative phenomenon. Nothing is ever that simple or simple-minded in Shepard's work. In the presentation of his characters, guilt or innocence is irrelevant; what is important is personal motivations. Shepard is a student of human nature, not an arbiter of morality (*a la* Bennett). There are no innocents in his fictional worlds, and those worlds are always fallen. The best that his characters can do is, through personal courage, perhaps with the help of their friends or allies, move a few degrees in the direction of an unattainable state of grace or faith. In this sense his fictions perfectly mirror life.

The "floater" of the title refers to a medical condition wherein the patient suffers from the build up of certain proteins in the iris of the eye, causing tiny particles to obstruct the field of vision. The detective, Dempsey, Shepard's protagonist, happens to contract this problem directly after being involved in the Diallo-like massacre of a character by the name of Lara. With this in mind, not to ruin enjoyment of the suspense or divert from the pleasures of the mystery, one can, in due course, reflect upon the idea of "seeing" in this story. *Floater* is all about the way we see, about how a change in one's world-view can literally transform one's reality.

I want to be careful not to reveal too much about the work you are about to read, but allow me to close by mentioning a thing or two about its creator. I had the good luck to meet Shepard in the autumn of 2002 in a hotel bar in Minneapolis. We were the only two in the place and it was early; all they were serving was coffee. Somehow we got to talking and I joined him at his table.

Rarely are writers, when you meet them in person, very representative of their work. I know that look of disappointment when I meet people who have enjoyed my books. Shepard, though, is the rare exception. He is a calm, good-natured, and good-humored conversationalist. The tales of his journeys and adventures in Honduras, on the Mosquito Coast, of his covering boxing for *Ring* Magazine, of his time spent riding the rails with contemporary Hobos, made it clear to me finally why his fictional settings and their detail are so unusually powerful. Few U.S. writers can convincingly portray the Third World like Shepard, because few have ever taken the time to experience it. It was obvious that he had lived what he had written about. Evident that morning also was the sense of humor that I had first taken notice of in the *Event Horizon* essay, and which manifests itself in nearly all of his fiction. In speaking of the career of the boxer, Roy Jones Jr., or current national politics, or the drug cartels in Honduras, or even the writing life, Shepard's take always transcended simple black-and-white determinations in favor of a factual complexity grappling with real understanding.

Now, onward to *Floater*. I hope you enjoy it as much as I did. More important than all of my musings above: it's a damn fine horror story.

Jeffrey Ford
May, 2003

FLOATER

DEMPSEY HATED THE MORNINGS before his drugs kicked in. Waking thick-headed and woozy from drink, with his eyelids stuck together, thoughts ensnared by the memory of some fugitive guilt-driven dream. Then the first gray seepage of light, the first unsteady steps, stumbling into the bathroom to piss, staring out the window, seeing, not Eleventh Street in February, but the tangle of tremulous dark lines and shifting opacities that had invaded his left eye. The ophthalmologist told him not to worry—it was only a floater. Microscopic scraps of protein adrift in the humor that cast shadows onto the retina. Yet over the course of a month it had evolved from scarcely more than a speck to an archipelago of cell-like structures that troubled half his field of vision. This, the ophthalmologist said, did not fall within the range of normal expectations. In the police shrink's opinion Dempsey's obsessiveness was making things worse. First the shooting incident, then the trial. Considering the pressures he'd been under, the shrink said, it would be an upset if he hadn't acquired a twitch or two. Dempsey wanted to accept these explanations. He wore the eye patch the ophthalmologist prescribed and, following the shrink's advice, he went on sick leave. But the floater was maddening and neither the patch nor lying around the apartment brought the least improvement. He came to believe the thing was an affliction sent by God, a malignancy seeded by his sinful act, and developed the paranoid conviction that it was extruding threads deeper into the jelly of the eye, into his brain. Unable to sleep, he took to washing down muscle relaxants with shots of vodka. His girl-friend Elise had done her best to support him; but phone calls from the press, death threats, his fits of despondency, and—ultimately—the trial, had finished them. She moved in with a friend. Temporarily, she said. Without her, he relied more heavily on the pills, the vodka, and came to hate everything about his life.

Thursday morning, three weeks into his leave, Dempsey fell out on the sofa to watch some tube. Vodka bottles, many lying on their side, littered the coffee table. Sections of newspapers ridged up along the fold, like the roofs of collapsed barns, carpeted the floor. A film of dust on the television screen caused *Gilligan's Island* to acquire the grainy appearance of vintage newsreel footage. Dempsey switched over to CNN. They were showing his academy photo again, slotted above the anchorman's right shoulder. Idiot-proud in his dress blues. Now, six years later, he thought he looked at least fifteen years older. Pinero's photograph materialized above the anchorman's other shoulder. They flanked him—good conscience, bad conscience. Pinero was also wearing his blues, striking a pose that made his jowly, acne-scarred face seem an imperious ideal that deserved commemoration on a coin. There followed a live shot of Haley, a skeletal, haunted version of his former self, talking with a tailored brunette who held a mike to his mouth and nodded with practiced sincerity at every lie and platitude. Dempsey tried to turn up the volume to hear what he was saying, but he fumbled the remote, and by the time he got it working, Haley had been replaced by a shot of the anchorman:

"Since NYPD Detectives Philip Pinero, Evan Haley, and William Dempsey were acquitted in the shooting death of immigrant street vendor Israel Lara, public outcry refuses to die down. Lara, who was shot twenty-six times in front of his apartment door when the detectives mistook his cell phone for a weapon, has become the symbol of a movement..."

The anchorman continued his voiceover as the screen switched to a shot of a sidewalk crowded with angry black and

Hispanic men and women, some holding posters depicting Lara's smiling dark face; then the camera focused on a rotund black man (with James Brown hair) in a pin-striped suit.

"...that continues to gain momentum. The Reverend Calvin Monckton today called for the governor to extend his investigation of police corruption to include the mayor's special Crime Action Teams, the CATs as they're known to most New Yorkers. Or, as they've come to be known to the residents of Fort Washington..."

The anchorman left a dramatic pause.

"...the Death Squads..."

Dempsey thumbed the channel button. Regis Philbin popped into view on-screen. He was breaking up his blond co-host again, mugging in a Green Bay Packer Cheesehead hat. Dempsey would have liked to kidnap his jaunty leprechaun ass, convey him to a deserted island, and hunt him for sport. He plucked a half-full bottle from the coffee table and had a swallow. Then he switched off the sound and channel-surfed until he landed on MTV. Brittany was shaking her denim-covered booty and lip-synching her heart out. Dempsey thought that he, Haley, and Pinero were on TV as much as Brittany these days, nearly as much as the damn mayor. Maybe they would all meet at the Emmys.

He picked up the phone, flirting with the notion of calling Elise, but nodded off and woke to the phone ringing in his lap. Startled, he dropped the receiver onto the floor, retrieved it and said thickly, "Yeah...hello? Hello?"

"You sound fucked up. Are you fucked up?"

"Haley?"

A silence, then Haley said, "Answer me, man! Are you fucked up?"

Dempsey did a stoned surfer voice. "It's all relative, dude."

"Can't you answer a simple goddamn question? Jesus fucking Christ!"

Dempsey told him, yeah, he was fucked up. Why the hell was it so important?

"The eye thing. It's not getting any better?"

"I don't think so."

Dempsey heard faint traffic noises through the phone. "Where are you?"

"It's worse, isn't it?"

"Maybe a little. I don't know. What's going on?"

"Nothing. I...I just wanted to know how you're doing."

Labored breathing. "I gotta go."

Haley hung up.

Infuriated, Dempsey punched in Haley's number, intending to ask what his goddamn problem was, but either Haley wasn't answering or he had turned off his phone. He tried the precinct. The desk sergeant told him Haley was still on sick leave. Dempsey stuffed the phone beneath the cushion and sat trying to calm his heart. He was freaking out, Haley was freaking out. Not Pinero, though. Pinero was taking things in stride. Fuck, he loved it. Every time he came on TV he acted as if he were running for Congress on the hate crime ticket. Because Lara was his Fort Washington homey, he had received something of a pass on guilt from the media and the citizens who vilified Haley and Dempsey. If they knew Pinero, Dempsey thought, if they spent fifteen minutes with him in a bar, on a stake-out, anywhere he'd show his true colors, they would not be so forgiving.

The sky above Brooklyn looked like the black and gray mess at the bottom of his ashtray. Darts of sleet streaked the windows, blurring the brownstones and the leafless trees outside. Dempsey wasn't hungry, but decided it would be wise to eat something. He headed down the stairs, contemplating pork sandwiches at the Cuban place on Seventh Avenue, but changed his mind, bought a dozen bagels from the Bagel Hole and drove into Manhattan. Sharing the food with the squad room, hanging out for a while...that would put him into a different head. But after parking across from the precinct, he remained in the car, listening to Bob Marley, watching uniforms pass in and out the entrance. He felt uncomfortable this close to his brothers in blue. Cut off

· 6 ·

from them by a barrier not of their making, but of his own. He reached into his jacket, groping for the pills.

A pounding on his window.

Startled, he saw Pinero peering in, bent over, holding the collar of his overcoat closed. Pinero made a twirling gesture, signaling him to roll down the window, and once this was done, he said angrily, "What, are you fucking zoned out again? Where you going?"

Dempsey said, "Just sitting, y'know."

"Jesus, Billy." Shaking his head in dismay, Pinero walked round the front of the car and climbed in the passenger side, bringing with him a smell of cigars and aftershave. He was two inches shorter than Dempsey, maybe thirty pounds heavier, but nonetheless Dempsey felt dwarfed, squeezed against the door, as if Pinero's presence was gigantic, an irresistible force. His black hair was wavy, shiny, like the hair of a porcelain saint.

"Sitting here like a fucking zombie. Listening to this dreadlock crap." Pinero switched off the CD player. "You making me look bad." He noticed the sack of bagels resting on the seat, opened it and chose a poppyseed. He tore it in half and chewed off a bite, his jaws working as he stared at Dempsey. "Go home, Billy."

"I figured the guys..." Dempsey's hand fluttered over the bagels. "They might wanta take a break."

"What're you? The Welcome Wagon? I'll carry 'em in for ya." Pinero cradled the sack in his lap. "Go home. Get yourself straight."

He had another bite, chewed stolidly. It seemed that his stare was microwaving Dempsey, heating him from the inside out, kindling anger and resentment.

"I don't get it," Dempsey told him. "It's like this whole thing's been massive for you. Like shooting a sorry motherfucker waved his phone at us was a goddamn..."

"Don't you talk!"

"...a goddamn photo op!"

"Don't you talk, man! Don't you pretend to know how I feel!" Pinero pounded the sack of bagels against the dash. "Just 'cause I'm not gimping it up like you and Haley doesn't mean I'm not having to deal with shit!"

"Yeah, I can see you're an emotional wreck!"

"Lara was an honest mistake. It sucked, but what you gonna do?"

"Boy, it musta really sucked for Lara. All the stuff spilling outa him, they probably buried him in shrinkwrap."

"Some bullets were yours, Billy."

"I thought you saw the gun, man! I thought you fucking saw it!"

Pinero screwed up his face, pinched his voice into that of a weepy child. "'I thought you saw the gun.' Jesus! What a pussy! Mister Billy 'Jet Li' Dempsey. The kung fu master! The badass street cop! Those *cabrones* on TV...you letting 'em get to you. Letting 'em make you into a sick little girl. That's not going to happen with me, man. 'Cause I faced what I done."

"Bullshit!"

"I faced what I done! I'm living with it! You did the same, you wouldn't hafta go round looking like Billy fucking Bones. You could put this shit behind you." Pinero's eyes drifted toward the entrance of the precinct house—three uniforms were standing on the steps, talking and laughing, their breath smoking. "You're still a Jersey boy. You don't understand the city. They on us now, that's for sure. They on our ass good. But somebody blows something up or the yos come busting outa Harlem in a bad mood, they gonna be begging to buy us bullets. Next week, next month, next year...it'll all be over. That's what you need to put your mind on. You gotta take hold of yourself. I was you I'd pull that fucking patch off and deal with the problem, not try and hide from it."

Dempsey was unclear as to how Pinero had managed to shift the conversation from an argument into a counseling session, but it had worked. He couldn't find his anger anymore.

"Tell you another thing." Pinero dropped his voice in pitch and volume as if confiding a secret. "Lara wasn't the happy innocent fuck they been selling on TV." He fielded Dempsey's sharp look with a nod. "No bullshit. I been poking around. He was a wrong guy."

"What? He sold a little grass or some shit?"

"It's nothing like that." Pinero tore off another bite; the bagel lumped his cheek as he chewed.

"Probably half those street guys down on Canal are humping some angle. That doesn't mean they need to get fucking shot."

Pinero shrugged, chewed.

"What you got?"

"*Santeria*," Pinero said.

"Aw, Christ!" Dempsey turned to face the traffic. A Metro bus passed by; Spiderman's enormous, impassive face gazed at him from the banner on its side.

"I'm not talking 'bout old ladies buying herbs and candles at the local botanica. I'm talking blood cults, man. Deep voodoo. Those storefront churches in Fort Washington, there's some evil shit goes on. Lara, he's all mixed up in it."

"Right," said Dempsey with a pale laugh.

"You don't know these things. I know 'em from when I'm a kid on Hunnerd-Seventy-First Street. Weird things happen you mess with these people. I've seen guys wither away in a coupla weeks, they get on the bad side of a *mambo*." Pinero struck his forehead with his knuckles, as if to punish himself. "Jeez, man! Sorry. Forget what I just said. I don't want you getting all fucked up worrying 'bout the thing with your eye's 'cause of a voodoo curse!"

It took Dempsey a few ticks to absorb this, to realize that Pinero had been playing him.

"Way you been acting, you liable to start hearing spirit drums," Pinero went on. "Seeing Lara's ghost pointing at you with his eyes all white."

"Get the fuck out!"

"Lighten up! I'm just trying to give you some perspective."

"You wanna go for a fucking ride?" Dempsey keyed the ignition. "Here we go."

Pinero opened the door. "You need to be dealing with this, Billy. The shrink, the doctors…they'll mess with your mind. They'll have you using a crutch the rest of your fucking life. Lose the patch. Face up to what's troubling you. It's the only way to fly." He climbed out, started to close the door, then ducked his head back in and held up the sack of bagels. "You didn't bring any cream cheese, didja?"

)(

THE CUBIST EXHIBITION at the Museum of Modern Art, Dempsey discovered, took on a nicely absurd aspect when you viewed it one-eyed. After sitting for half an hour on a bench in front of a Picasso, he began to picture himself as the subject of a Gary Larson cartoon, a clownish-looking guy with one eye and a jagged sideways face staring at the Blue Period portrait for which he'd modeled. He stood a while in the atrium, swallowed a couple of pills, and watched Elise moving among the tables, her brown hair flipping up from her shoulders with every step, bringing cappuccino and pastries to the art lovers. He gave thought to going over and sitting in her section, but remained where he was, hidden behind a column.

Around two o'clock he left the museum, drove down into the East Village. He wandered around awhile, checking out shop windows, then dropped into the Hollywood Lounge, a dive bar a block off St. Mark's Square, set in kind of a half basement. Except for the bartender, a tanned, stocky man in his 50s with pomaded gray hair and a square Eastern European face, the place was empty. Dempsey sat at the end of the bar, his back to a wooden screen behind which lay a dozen or so booths, and smoked half a pack of Camel Wide Lights while drinking two beers, watching a soccer match showing soundlessly on the TV mounted on the wall. In the dimness the digital beer ads back of the counter gleamed like distant nebulas whenever he let his vision go out of focus. He was soothed by traffic noise and the clinking of glassware. Maybe Pinero had a point, he told himself.

Maybe he was looking for a crutch. Maybe he did need to deal straightforwardly with the situation. He wasn't sure about losing the patch, though. He'd taken a peek before entering the bar and it was almost as if a spider had spun a web across his eye.

Two men came in, one close upon the heels of the other—a gaunt, lanky Jewish-looking guy in his late forties, wearing a brown raincoat and a sardonic expression, and a Latino man with a round cheerful face, early thirties, dressed in jeans and a bulky yellow sweater. After ordering an Old Fashioned, the Latino complained to the bartender about his business difficulties. He supplied transvestite performers for parties and had been stiffed on some recent contracts, a circumstance he outlined with a degree of self-deprecation. The bartender, whose name proved to be Roland, advised him to find new employment.

"No offense," he said. "But those people...they're not exactly the most stable individuals."

"I know, I know!" The Latino man stirred his drink and shook his head ruefully.

The lanky guy ordered a beer and asked Roland to switch to CNN and bring up the sound.

"You want the news?" Roland said as he changed channels. "Same as yesterday. You got the priests banging the choirboys, the Middle East, and Bush did some stupid shit."

"He waved at Stevie Wonder," said the Latino man. "Did you see that?"

"Fuck the news," the lanky guy said. "I just like that blond they got on in the afternoon."

"Stevie's blind and Bush waves at him!" Ignored by the others, the Latino man looked to Dempsey for support and Dempsey returned a weak smile.

"She's okay." Roland set out a coaster and put the man's beer on it. "But her voice reminds me of my ex's terrier. The one I like's that skinny dark-haired broad's on in the morning."

"Daryn!" The Latino guy placed a hand on his heart and shut his eyes as if in rapture. "She's gorgeous!"

"Daryn...yeah. What's her last name?"

"Kagan."

"That's it. Daryn Kagan."

Dempsey had the urge to nominate a CNN weatherwoman, Jaqui Jeras, for sexual icon, but the conversation shifted gears and they began to talk about how the neighborhood had gone to hell, all the yuppies moving in, the businesses changing. Roland was especially piqued by the bistro next door, which had once been an Italian restaurant.

"Know who goes there?" He included them all, even Dempsey, in the question. "Argentine lesbians. No shit. Kid works there told me it's the fucking center of the Argentine lesbian scene. That's what he called it. The Argentine lesbian scene."

"Niche marketing," said the lanky guy, grinning.

"What? Argentine lesbians can't hang with Rumanian lesbians? Brazilian lesbians? They have difficulty interacting? They each need their own fucking bistro?"

The lanky guy chuckled. "You need to compete, Roland. Call your place the Croatian Lesbians Lounge."

The Latino guy said it wasn't only the yuppies, it was the new style of depravity, and described having seen two men masturbating on a tree trunk in Washington Square. In broad daylight.

The lanky guy raised an eyebrow. "And you were shocked?"

Roland tapped the counter. "Here's your blond."

The anchorwoman's adenoidal voice imbued the Kashmiri crisis with the emotional value of a Tupperware infomercial. Roland tuned her down to a mutter. The third story she spoke to was the aftermath of the Lara trial. The screen displayed a clip shot at the courthouse in Albany, the three of them on the steps: Pinero beaming, Haley with his zombie stare, and Dempsey gaping at something off-camera. This was followed by a live shot of 164th Street in Fort Washington. Yet another protest. Dempsey lowered his gaze to the countertop and understood that he could not be a cop any longer. This did not seem a conclusion, the sum of doubt and long reflection, because until that second he had assumed he would remain a cop. The thought simply occurred to him, as if by dropping his head he had shifted a liquid level in his brain and revealed the promontory of a new understanding. He had no idea what he might do instead, but rooting through dumpsters for pop cans would be less stressful. For the moment he was made hopeful by the prospect of cutting loose from that paranoid, corrupt, heroic world whose citizens were at the mercy of their own confusions as much as, if not more than, the people they were sworn to protect.

He glanced up and saw himself on TV, talking to the same cute brunette who interviewed Haley, and recalled the perfumed ambition steaming off her, the glossiness of her hair. He noticed the other three men staring at him. The lanky guy and Roland turned away, but it appeared the Latino man was bursting to say something. He dug for his wallet, but his eyes kept darting toward Dempsey. He dropped bills on the counter and said, "I gotta get back. See you guys tomorrow." With an openly hostile glance at Dempsey, he made for the door.

"That guy!" said the lanky man, and made a disparaging noise. "He's a fucking mess."

"Man pays his tab, never causes any trouble," Roland said. "Far as I'm concerned he's a *mensch*."

Dempsey stood, reached into his pocket, and Roland, with some hesitation, said, "Don't feel you hafta go, officer. Okay? Lemme getcha a cold one."

"Damn right!" The lanky guy swiveled about to face him. "You guys got our support."

The support of these solid citizens would make all the difference, Dempsey thought. It would clean away the emotional sediment and allow him to see the purity of what they had done, the dutiful honesty of their bloody mistake. Fucking A. He sat back down, not because he cared to bask in the approval of the right-wing proletariat, but because he felt light-headed and heavy in the legs. He drank the beer, letting the lie of their acceptance smooth him out. This was not really an approval thing, he reminded himself. He was possessed of a damaged notoriety, a perfect source for anecdotal material. He could almost hear Roland telling someone, "Know who come in this afternoon? One of those cops blew away the PR in Fort Washington. Motherfucker was toasted."

After another beer he went into the bathroom and took a leak. As he washed up he stared at his reflection and tentatively lifted the patch. The floater was no smaller, but the lines had stopped trembling. Weird. They seemed to have settled into a pattern. Like he was seeing a pencil sketch of a diminishing perspective. He focused on the lines. It looked, he decided, sort of like a corridor. He could make out doorways ranging it, the molding along the ceiling. He covered his right eye and turned his head slightly to discover how this would affect his sight. It appeared the sketch surrounded him, that he had turned inside it and now was facing a door. Intricately detailed. A knob and a peephole, a broken number hanging cockeyed. All composed of fine black lines. A cold sensation washed into his groin. He recognized the number: 126. Bits of protein in the humor... Fuck that noise! Bits of protein didn't arrange themselves into an artist's rendering of a corridor.

Not this corridor.

A wash of whiteness obscured some of the lines that comprised the ceiling; then a second white streak was smeared across part of a wall, as though someone with an artist's brush were painting over the sketch one stroke at a time, working fast, and Dempsey, seeing that somehow the lines had expanded to enmesh all his vision, left *and* right eye, understood that if this kept up, he would not be able to see anything. Within seconds there was so much white, it seemed he was peeking at the bathroom through a white bush, glimpsing portions of the mirror, his affrighted face, the peeling paint on the wall. He pressed the patch to his eye, but that was no help. The invisible artist was working faster. A few more swipes of the brush would blind him. Dempsey rubbed at his eyes, trying to shake something up, disperse those bits of protein. He pressed his face to the mirror, half-expecting to detect a white film seeping over the eye, but it was clear and blue, without apparent defect.

The instant before this white darkness became complete, Dempsey had a sickening feeling. The kind you get when you realize you've lost control of a car or the rope you've been hanging from has snapped, or you step into the street and catch a glimpse of something huge hurtling toward you. You feel a dreamlike paralysis, a suspension in light, as if God or somebody is snapping a polaroid just before you go spinning, sinking, falling into terror and darkness...or, if you were Dempsey, stumbling along a darkened corridor that seemed to melt up from the whiteness, hearing muffled music from somewhere close by, a man's voice speaking peremptorily, English words that he couldn't understand, and he turned toward the voice, slowly because he was drunk, and saw three shadows in the alcove beneath the broken ceiling fixture and lifted a hand in fearful reflex as a flash erupted from one of the shadows, something slammed him against the wall, and then it was all flashes and roaring noise, and he was down and the air was full of uncoiling smoke, he tasted blood in his mouth, and he tried to speak, to say a name and pass what he carried to the shadow leaning over him, but his lungs were filling as if he were drowning in a warm sea, a fluid thicker than water...

How could he be drowning?

Dempsey found he was gripping the edge of the sink, breathing raggedly, half his feelings and thoughts still trapped in Israel Lara's skin. He was frightened, but his fear was trumped by the implausibility of what had happened. Yet he would swear under oath that it *had* happened. Logically, it was shaky. Very shaky. But he had smelled cordite, felt the impact of the bullets, and—most pertinently—he had a sense of Lara, as if the man were a liquid that had been poured into him and now that he had been poured out, a residue remained. Maybe what Pinero said about Lara being a wrong guy wasn't so far-fetched, because Dempsey detected a flavor of mean-spiritedness, a grasping nature...

Jesus!

He smacked the wall with the heel of his hand. Where was his fucking head? Lara was dead. Dead twenty-six times over. Holding his left eye shut, he squinted at his reflection. He looked shaken, but saw no twitches, no drool, no sign of having lost it. Though it was plain he had lost it for a minute. He opened the eye. The sketch of the corridor was no longer in evidence. Just opaque blobs and dark tangles. He cast about for his patch. Spotted it on the tile floor, soaking in fluid beneath the urinal. He 'd have to hit a pharmacy and pick up another one. And then what? Go back to the apartment and watch TV until he passed out? Call the shrink? The shrink would boost his meds. That would buy him a better high. Not inconsequential, but he was sick of pills. He needed something to take his mind off the trial, the shooting, his eye. He didn't want to go back to work. They'd stick him on a desk and he'd be in the same boat, bored and unhappy, only without any TV.

Suppose he hadn't been tripping just now?

I mean there was a chance. Slim, but you couldn't ignore it. Shit like this happened. Jesus' face appears on aluminum siding, somebody falls from an airplane and lives. The Patriots win the Super Bowl.

Suppose he'd actually experienced Lara's death and what he had felt was not delirium, not a psychotic break, not the drugs. Suppose it was due to *santeria*. Lara's voodoo revenge from beyond the grave. A curse laid by a relative, a friend. Embracing this ludicrous proposition would give him something to do. Pinero's joke about his eye problems being the result of a voodoo curse...it might not have been a joke. Pinero was a strange guy. A cop with independent means. Some people in the department claimed he liked being a cop too much, but they refused to expand upon this. Watch your ass, they'd told him. Just watch your ass. Everything Pinero had said was probably designed to provoke him, nothing more. But it was worth going over the case file, anyway. Check if Lara had been involved in *santeria*. Ask a few questions. He could stay on leave and do his own investigation. Playing cop used to cure his boredom when he was a kid. Who knows what he might find? Odds were good that this was no more than a pathological symptom, a new level of freak-out.

But what if it had really happened?

H

ACCORDING TO THE CASE FILE the investigating officers had run a background check on Lara, doubtless hoping to discover something to justify the shooting, but had come up with no evidence of malfeasance. Dempsey noticed that one of the interviewees, Sara Pichardo, gave her address as the Ellegua Botanica on 172nd Street. That sounded like voodoo to Dempsey. In the neighborhood where Lara had been killed, someone was certain to recognize him, no matter how well he disguised himself; but risk was unavoidable. He strapped on his shoulder holster and a heavy windbreaker, a Rangers cap, and pasted a fake tattoo of a bar code on the side of his jaw. He still looked like the photo the *Post* had run under the headline KILLER COPS INNOCENT, but he thought it would take more than a casual glance to identify him.

In reflex he reached for his pills. He started to pop off the cap, but set the vial on the kitchen counter and, shedding his jacket, made coffee and toast. Better not to be feeling like Gumby when he might have to make quick moves. He ate on the sofa, watching Chuck Norris and Lee Marvin in *Delta Force* without the sound. The movie was just beginning and Dempsey was tempted to do a couple of shots, couple of blue pills, lie back and driftily watch Chuck and Lee kick some terrorist ass. Forget all this cowboy bullshit he'd been considering,

The phone rang.

He picked up and said, "You got me."

"You sound better, Billy. Been laying off the downs?" Pinero.

"Fuck do you want?"

"I got bad news, but you need to hear it. Haley's dead."

Dempsey couldn't speak.

"He ate his gun over in Prospect Park," Pinero said. "Last night sometime. I don't know the details."

Dempsey had a screwloose feeling, like that he had experienced when he blew out his knee playing high school ball and heard the sound of cartilage popping issue from inside his body. The phone call, he thought. The way Haley had talked.

"Still with me, Billy?"

"He called me yesterday."

"Haley? What did he say?"

"He asked how I was doing. He was all wired and..." A hot pressure built inside Dempsey's head, as if a circuit were frying. He squeezed his eyes shut. "Shit!"

"You okay?

"I kinda blew him off. Jesus!"

"Don't pussy out on me. The man ate his gun. Nothing you did was gonna stop it."

The beginnings of shock flipped over into anger and Dempsey said, "The hell should I do? Give a fucking interview? That always brightens your outlook!"

"You wanna feel responsible for every shit thing that happens? Go for it, *chico*! You be walking the same road as Haley."

"Fuck you!"

"You know, I told the captain day you come on the squad, I said this motherfucker thinks like a goddamn woman. All sensitive and shit. See his file? His papi teaches college. He's got a sister named Madison, for God's sakes. What's that about? Send his ass over to homicide, I said. It's his fucking wet dream, anyway. Let him go play mastermind with all those other fruitbars think they rule the world."

Inarticulate with rage, Dempsey pounded the receiver against the sofa cushion. When he put it to his ear once again, Pinero was saying, "...long before he makes a mistake gets us all dead."

"You got that wrong, didn't you?" Dempsey said, more in control. "It wasn't me who fucked up."

"You think *I* made a mistake?"

"What else would you call it?"

"I call it justice with a bang. One dead criminal motherfucker and three live cops."

Suddenly drained, Dempsey let the seconds roll past.

"Your mistake's still ahead of you," Pinero said. "But I don't want you to make it, Billy. I need you to stay alive."

Dempsey spat out a laugh. "What? You're concerned for me?"

"I don't even like you, man."

"Then why the fuck do you care?"

"I got my reasons," said Pinero, and hung up.

⨯

TWO BLOCKS OFF BROADWAY, 172nd Street, *cumbia* rhythms leaked from the Rosa Del Sol music shop, a *merengue* fluttered from a second story window, a son pulsed from a car radio. Even in winter the place had the residual feeling of a tropic, albeit one polluted by gangs and crack and city paranoia. The projects—ochre monoliths that sprang up several blocks farther along and spread into the 160s—were a felony theme park, a breeding ground for Pineros and worse. They were part of the city, part of the smoke-gray emotion that governed it. But despite flakes of snow falling from the dirty sky, here where the buildings were two and three stories, the music and brightly painted facades, people calling out in Spanish, the camaraderie that seemed to exist, all this made it possible for Dempsey to imagine that he was walking down a street in Aguadilla, hibiscus blooming close by, coco palms waving, brown-skinned kids in shorts kicking a soccer ball. It was one of those rare places that had maintained a separate, buoyant identity, somehow managing to avoid being swallowed up by the fugue that had descended over Manhattan during the last part of the previous century, a fugue that the delusional claimed no longer existed, but in reality had only moved uptown, banished there by the equally oppressive spirit of commerce. Haley had called the area the Beach and shared Dempsey's affection for it. Because of this and other such correspondences, Dempsey had once thought they might become friends. They'd tried it a time or two. Gone out for beers, caught a Yankee game, dinner with the girlfriends. But there had been a fundamental mistrust between them. Dempsey had assumed this was because Haley was more like Pinero than he was, more suited to police culture; but now that Haley had displayed his vulnerability by killing himself, most likely in reaction to the shooting, Dempsey suspected that the reverse might be true.

Eleggua Botanica was a dignified little storefront with a freshly painted white facade and gilt lettering on its windows, which displayed a number of ritual objects, many apparently antiques, neatly arranged on dark green cloth. The iron security gate was half-closed, preventing both easy access and a quick exit. A bell jingled as he pushed inside and an attractive young Latina wearing a bulky cardigan over a print dress, her long black hair tied with a blue ribbon, emerged from behind a curtain at the rear and stood by a display counter, hands clasped at her belly, looking at him with a neutral expression. Except for the two of them, the botanica was empty. It was a small space, made smaller by cabinets and bookshelves and stands holding statuary, jars with handwritten labels, objects fashioned of bone, shells, feathers, brass. There was an odd sweetish smell, not altogether pleasant, musty and thick—the sort of smell, Dempsey thought, that had taken a great long while to accumulate and was likely compounded of a thousand lesser smells, some altogether unpleasant.

"Sara Pichardo?" he asked.

The woman nodded and he said, "I'd like to ask you a couple questions."

"Police?" She drew out the last syllable, lending the word an inappropriate delicacy.

He showed his badge and she shrugged in assent. With someone else, he might have taken her lack of volubility as reluctance or outright recalcitrance, but he had from her an impression of calm reserve and suspected this was her way with everyone.

"You knew Israel Lara, right?"

"He came in the shop several times. Once to inquire about the church and..."

"What church is that?"

"The church of Lukumi Babalu Aye. It's on Hundred-Sixty-Fifth and Eighth."

"He was a practitioner of *santeria*?"

A worry line marked her brow. "I told this to the police. Twice now."

"Twice?"

"Yes. After Lara was shot, and then a few days ago."

"The police were here a few days ago? Detectives?"

"One detective."

"Do you remember his name?"

"No, but he was Puerto Rican."

Pinero? Doing some poking around?

Dempsey started to ask another question, but was interrupted by a cracked high-pitched voice from the rear of the shop calling, "Sara!"

"*Momentito*," Sara said, and hurried back behind the curtain.

Left alone, Dempsey had a look round. His eye was caught by a statue of dark wood in a corner cabinet: a squat, frowning man about two feet high with large pupil-less eyes, froglike features, ropes about his neck, arms spread in what Dempsey perceived to be a hopeless gesture. The style of carving and pale brown wood made it seem like Caribbean work. Maybe South American. On closer inspection, he decided the figure was not a man but an anthropomorphic fish creature. The eyes were fashioned from mother-of-pearl; the ropes were strands of shells. An ancient green Mercury with a Puerto Rican flag spraypainted on the driver's side passed on the street, a speaker blasting congas, trumpets, guitars. When Dempsey turned back to the statue, it appeared to have increased in malevolence, as if aggravated by the music. He stretched out a finger to touch the statue, but a twinge of superstition, of leeriness, caused him to pull back.

"I'm sorry," said Sara Pichardo, coming back into the room, once more positioning herself by the display case. "My great-grandmother needed something."

She appeared to be studying his face. Dempsey stepped closer to her. "So was Lara into *santeria*?"

"He was a Shango Baptist."

Dempsey remarked that he'd never heard the term and she said, "*Santeria* is more African than Christian. What the Baptists believe is more Christian than African. Just a little. They're very close. Brother and sister." She took a pack of cigarillos from a pocket of the cardigan, tapped one out, and lit up; she exhaled a stream of smoke and watched it hang on the air. "Lara couldn't find a church he liked, so he asked about mine. It happens a lot. People come from the south and discover the feeling's different here. They switch back and forth."

"Sounds like you talked to him a lot."

"People come in, I talk to them. I even talk to the police."

She gave a half-smile and he realized that though it didn't jump out at you, she was exotic-looking. It was her stillness, he thought, that disguised the fact. All her gestures and expressions seemed constrained, yet he had the idea this wasn't due to repression, but was evidence of composure. There was a comfortable quality to her poise that made him think she had acquired it through service or discipline. Her eyes were large, slanted a bit, and her face, with its prominent cheekbones and firm mouth, tapered severely to a small chin. She wore no make-up he could detect and her loose clothing hid her figure. That by design, he figured.

He asked further questions, not interested in answers as much as in watching her shape them, listening more to the modulations of her voice. He had the idea she was also watching, listening. A humming came to his ears, some internal process amplified by a tension between them. Not sexual. He felt nothing of that from her. Hers was a pointed interest, like his own. He asked why Lara came to her for information about the church. Because she ran the botanica?

"It's my church. But I think he was interested in me."

"Okay...I got it."

"No, not that way. He wanted to learn how strong I was." She broke off, folded her arms, looked down at the display case; then, lifting her eyes, she said, "I know you."

Dempsey, as if a spell had been broken, felt suddenly distant from her, stranded in his briefly forgotten guilt and confusion.

Sara held her hands up in a placating gesture. "I recognize you, but that's not what I mean. I know about your eye. What's happening to you."

Here it comes, he told himself. The scam, the hustle.

"You're at the center of a struggle between two forces," she said. "One is trying to kill you, the other's using you. Whichever prevails, there's a good chance you'll die."

Dempsey bit back a laugh. "And you know this how?"

"You want me to say things that will make you laugh at me? Or you want me to help you understand them?"

"That's my choice? Gee, that's a toughie."

Disregarding this, she said, "Your choice is to be a fool or to trust me. To live or die." She turned to a shelf behind her, took down a glass vial filled with dark powder and handed it to Dempsey. "Make a tea of this tonight. Drink it all and come to me tomorrow night. Ten o'clock. At the church."

"You mean the church of Lukumoo Babayama...whatever."

He expected her to become angry, but she folded her arms again, tipped her head to the side. "Yes. I'm the *mambo*...the priestess."

Dempsey weaved his shoulders, made dance moves with his arms. "Is this like a salsa clinic you're running? Mambo, cha cha cha."

Again she failed to rise to the bait. "You need to be very careful. Someone is trying to hurt you. Someone close."

"You got the all-seeing eye, huh? Things just pop out at you."
A shrug.

"How much is this going to cost?" he asked.

"Whatever the price," she said as if announcing a sad fact, "you may not be able to pay it."

Her poise seemed to be acting upon him, calming him, yet even so, he felt himself beginning to unravel, as if it were his anger that was holding him together. Yet anger and cynicism weren't part of the program. He'd set himself to work this like a real case, accepting the implausible, the ridiculous, and the purely venal at face value.

"Things are like you say," he asked, "why would you help me?"

She hesitated. "It's in my best interests."

"That's a little vague."

She rubbed the back of her neck and appeared to be thinking. "Whatever I tell you now will make it more difficult for you. You'll reject it, you'll struggle to maintain your view of the world. You need to come to this knowledge on your own. If you don't, then you won't let me help you." She laid a hand on her abdomen. "You *know* something bad is happening. You know it here." She shifted the hand to her forehead. "And here. Accept it. Feel where you are in the world. Think how you reached this point and about everything that happens between now and tomorrow night."

Dempsey turned his attention to the display case, to the sachets and bottles beneath the glass. "I come in here, ask some questions, and you take a look and see I've been cursed. That's a little hard to accept."

"It's not a curse."

"Uh-huh. But you're not going to tell me what it is 'cause if you do I won't believe it." He rapped a knuckle on the glass. "See, I'm not gonna buy this. It's too damn slick. Tell me something. You said I was in danger. Who from?"

"I already told you."

This answer had the same skewed bounce as had all the others. "Okay. Help me now. I don't want to wait."

"I have to prepare. So do you."

"How the fuck am I supposed to prepare?"

"Drink the tea."

He inspected the vial. The powder was tobacco brown, fine as flour.

"It's peonia," she said. "A herb given to initiates."

"Initiates. You gonna jump me into your church? I thought you were gonna fix my eye."

"One will lead to the other."

"What's in my eye? You should know, you're gonna fix it."

She made a fretful noise. "I'll tell you this much. Then you can laugh." Kids sailed by outside on rollerblades and she tracked them past the window. "A god named Olukun is looking at you. You have been brought to his notice. What you see in your eye is his eye, which sees everywhere. All you see now is the beginning of what he sees and what he is. In order to see what you must, you have to look deeper."

"And you're gonna teach me how."

"If you can open yourself to seeing, I will help you."

The way she stood there, beaming out that cool calm vibe, like a sexy New Age machine, an orgone silencer, a vortex inhibitor...it made him believe that she could actually help, though on another level he knew she was a fraud. Yet he wanted to believe that in a city where beautiful women understood their exact worth and used that knowledge to take from the men who took from them, there lived a beautiful woman who would volunteer salvation, perform magical operations, not just run the old psychic game of throwing out general statements and gauging your responses.

Not that he needed salvation.

He was in the clear, his actions validated by due process.

"I'm not laughing," he said.

"You will." She put a hand to the back of her hair, lowered her head and angled it to the side, that deferential, self-regarding pose that seems common to all women. "But tomorrow...maybe not."

♓

I T WAS A GOOD THING, Dempsey told himself as he drove the freeway, heading downtown, that he no longer wanted to be a cop, because while race, religion, and gender were purportedly not taken into account by one's superiors, he was fairly certain that joining a voodoo cult would not be deemed a career move by anyone associated with the NYPD. Make a hell of a comic book, though. Sergeant Shango. Blowing away the bad guys by feeding them their own pubic hair and cutting goat throats. Zombies in grave-rotted rags clambering from steaming manholes and calling his name in stuporous, thickened voices, only to shrivel away when they felt his bolts of unholy green fire. The cable TV spin-off would star some Hollywood loser, a B-list actor sunk to the level of weekly programming. Give him a comic sidekick. Tom Arnold or Andy Dick. Set it in an alternate-universe Manhattan after the ice caps had melted, skyscrapers sheathed in phosphorescent fungi and flesh-eating creepers. The streets black rivers afloat with skulls, aswim with fiendish carnivores. Ruled by that fishgod guy from the botanica, his eyes glowing like foxfire, belly sagging like a hundred-year-old hammock. For a logo, the night skyline mounted against an enormous blood moon and giant tentacles flailing above the Empire State Building, one holding the Statue of Liberty's head.

Swamp City.

Population: Who Knows, Who Cares.

Dempsey began to have that unraveling feeling again. He parked and went into a coffee shop a block off Lexington and

33rd, slumped into a booth and tried to puzzle things out. Forget that Sara Pichardo's generic warnings were a hustle. Accept what she said as fact. That was the assignment.

Fact One: He was at the center of a struggle between two opposing forces.

Fact Two: One side was using him, one was trying to kill him, and whichever side won, he would die.

Fact Three: Sara Pichardo wanted him to believe that she was trying to help him, so—unless she was dissembling—she represented neither force.

Fact Four: Someone close to him was a threat. Someone he knew.

Fact Five: Lara was not what he seemed. What the hell was Peonia? And let's not forget Olukun...

Number Four was the easiest to investigate. Few people were close to him. Elise was out, as was Haley. His family was scattered along the Jersey Shore. That left Pinero and the guys Dempsey played hoops with in Park Slope.

Which meant Pinero was it.

Sara Pichardo claimed she had told him who was threatening him and, since she implied that it wasn't Lara, it would have to be the detective who had interviewed her a few days earlier. Except for her great-grandmother, he was the only other person she had mentioned. Of course she had managed all this in such a way that he wound up supplying the answers to his own questions. That was the beauty of the hustle. But if she had perceived Pinero as a threat, wouldn't she have recognized him? Would she have mentioned it? No, she'd find a way to slide. She could say she hadn't yet recognized Dempsey's part in things and thus saw no reason to tell him. She'd say she was by her reticence encouraging him to work things out. Still, it might be a good idea to tail Pinero. Whether or not he was involved in a voodoo feud, he might have a couple of secrets worth knowing. Dempsey had not entertained the possibility that Pinero had acted for any other reason apart from an excess of zeal; but now, considering everything, was it so great a leap to conjecture that he had engineered Lara's execution? He'd been the one who spotted Lara entering his building, who asserted that Lara looked suspicious. He'd convinced them that the man posed a danger. They had been a tough sell—Haley, especially—but Pinero pushed and pushed. He was the first to open fire, the last to stop. He displayed a minimum of public remorse and none whatsoever in private. Dempsey reminded himself that his investigation was an exercise and that he would enjoy proving Pinero guilty of anything, especially if doing so would absolve him to a degree of his own guilt. Thus he distrusted his enthusiasm for the idea. He turned his eyes to the street, dimly registering passers-by, mesmerized by the fast-walking rhythms of men in overcoats and down jackets, immersed in an aimless, confusing depth, a bustling diorama of grays and dark blues interrupted now and again by the bloom of a woman's bright winter colors, the clatter and bash in the coffee shop adding a chaotic soundtrack to this half-glimpsed plane.

A waitress brought breakfast for two men in an adjacent booth and the smell of bacon called to Dempsey. For the first time in weeks he was hungry. He flagged another waitress and ordered bacon and eggs, a short stack, and juice. And a second order of bacon.

"How 'bout a side of cholesterol?" said the waitress, a sinewy, embittered woman in her late twenties. "You might as well go for the whole heart attack." She offered a brittle smile as if to imply that what she'd said was a joke, but Dempsey suspected vegetarian politics.

As he shoveled in the food he felt his levels boosting as rapidly as those of a character in a video game, his health going blue, strength graph charting to the top. Damn, he had an appetite! He hadn't felt so in-tune for months. He ate for almost a half-hour, paid the check, and drove toward Brooklyn. Once again he grudgingly credited Pinero for a good call. Confronting his problems, even in such an oblique fashion, was far better therapy than moping around the house. He switched on the CD player, drummed on the steering wheel in accompaniment to Burning Spear. Marcus Garvey. Jah Rastafari. Everything was irie in Dempsey's heart and he went skanking onto the Manhattan Bridge; but a hole was blown in his holy-ganja view of things when he realized that he hadn't been feeling this good until he talked with Sara Pichardo. As if her presence had a healing effect. The notion that this might be no coincidence, inferring that he might be involved with something too elusive to confront, reawakened him to the dismal term of his recent history, and by the time he came down onto the Brooklyn side, the light seemed the wan light of a winter battlefield and pedestrians moved at the pace of weary soldiers in the process of abandoning it and he was submerged again in an anxious mindset, anticipating nightmares and shadows and bad TV movies.

Haley, he said, not sounding the name, only shaping it as he settled into a honking traffic snarl along Seventh Avenue. Images of Haley summoned from his mental file flickered in and faded. He wondered what had been on Haley's mind and it occurred to him that Haley, too, might have been afflicted with a physical problem that had developed since the shooting. He might have made some connection between his trouble and Dempsey's floater. Thus the phone call. He'd been comparing notes and had learned nothing favorable. Dempsey could not reject the possibility, but at the moment he did not want to trivialize the death by braiding it into a crazy hypothesis. He fixed his thoughts on the traffic, on the neon script pizza joint mad cabby hip hop ambiance of millennial rush hour Brooklyn. White exhaust plumed from the cars, lifting into the sky like crematory smoke. Two black kids on the corner chested each other, then started hooking for real. An old gray-bearded tramp stood by the doorway of a bar, counting the change in his palm. Beside Dempsey, a bald man in a station wagon leaned his head out the window and cursed the world.

){

THE INTERNET, according to Dempsey's dad, an intellectual snob and curmudgeon, was variously "like having a sewer running through one's living room," "an evil addiction," and "a proving ground for the self-esteem of idiots." But it proved useful for Dempsey, providing him with information on peonia, an anti-spasmodic soothing to the nervous system, Olukun, the male/warrior aspect of the Supreme Being, Oludamare, and Shango Baptists. Depending on whom you believed, Shango Baptist was either an umbrella term used to denote a group of syncretic religions combining the beliefs of Christianity and voodoo—*santeria*, *candomble*, and so forth—or else it referred to a specific form of Christian animism that had arisen from the Aladura faith in Nigeria, and now, as practiced in Trinidad and Mexico, had incorporated elements of Asian religions as well. The only salient information that Dempsey derived from all this was that peonia would not poison him; though it did give some credibility to what Sara Pichardo had told him about Lara, since Lara—Puerto Rican by birth—had emigrated to the States from Trinidad. Dempsey looked up *santeria* on Google, found thousands of pages devoted to the subject, checked a few. One page was devoted to a woman named Maya Derens, an experimental filmmaker back in the Thirties who, it was claimed, had been the only Caucasian person ever possessed by a voodoo god. She referred to the experience as "the white darkness," a phrase that fascinated Dempsey, reminding him of his own. He looked up Maya Derens with the search engine and read excerpts from a book she had written on the subject, but it didn't seem relevant to the case and he moved on to other searches. Another site described the act of possession as being "ridden" and used the term "horses" for those who were possessed. He accessed a dozen more pages on *santeria*, but there was simply too much material to absorb and soon he gave it up.

Dempsey left his apartment at seven that evening and drove into the West Village. He parked down the street from a brownstone whose front steps were under repair, covered with tarps. Pinero habitually spent the early part of Friday night in a first floor apartment with his mistress—his SUV was parked half a block farther along. It had warmed up late in the day and a white mist had risen, investing the ordinary with a fey fragility, turning schlumps trudging home with a six pack under their arm into messengers from the East bearing sacred texts, blending the row of brownstones into the wing of a castle, softening the window lights into mysterious beacons. Couples holding hands and strolling vanished into luminous oblivion like lovers in a shadow play. Dempsey, a connoisseur of these city miracles, these urban counterfeits of natural beauty, had to force himself to concentrate on the matter at hand. For the better part of an hour he watched the brownstone alertly, noting every entrance and exit; but during the second hour his attention wandered and when Pinero emerged shortly after nine, wearing gray slacks and a tan leather jacket. Dempsey didn't spot him until he was about to unlock the SUV. Pinero waved at one of the windows. Blew a kiss. A Norman Rockwell portrayal of good ol' American infidelity.

Pinero passed the next hour in a pink frame house on the edge of Park Slope that had been remodeled and turned into a bar with no name, an establishment whose very namelessness proclaimed an ultra-egalitarian exclusivity, whose patrons were cool enough to sneer at themselves for pretending not to care that they were so cutting-edge. It wasn't the hangout Dempsey would have chosen for Pinero. Like most bars-with-no-name in New York

City, the atmosphere was dim smoky noisy. The aisles were packed. Tequila and wine were the drinks of choice and no one except Pinero looked older than their early thirties. Women were dressed for casual show in tight blouses and tighter jeans. A few men sported suits and loosened ties; most were scruffy-looking, but wielded cell phones and palm pilots. An art-yuppie crowd. Writers, painters, architects, performance artists with grants, a smattering of musicians whose bands, loose associations that lasted for months only, gigged exclusively at bars-with-no-name, delighting their quasi-trendy pre-bourgeois audiences with sardonic, inept post-rock. Out of about two hundred people, a mere handful were black, all men and all duded up in a fashion that presented a non-menacing credential. Silver pants, embroidered jackets, chrome hair. There were two bartenders, a third on stand-by. The one who served Dempsey—he had stationed himself near the door—was a tall dark-haired girl, extremely slender, bra-less under a tank top, with pale olive skin and a remarkably dramatic face, all long planes and arch, aquiline curves. Either dismayed by or reacting politically against the idea of natural beauty, she had redrawn her mouth in dark crimson, highlighted her eyes in rose, styled her hair into an upswept punky mess, and mutilated one eyebrow so that it resembled a series of dots and hyphens—in sum, a mask of cultivated unhealthiness that fell into the gap between mortician chic and the fashionably terminal. On her upper right arm was a tattoo of an antique vacuum cleaner, and on her left an antique toaster. Her ears were edged by half-a-dozen silver earrings each, making him think of snails clinging at the waterline of a tidepool, and while her face was free of piercings, the controlled suppleness of her hips as she pivoted between bottles and sinks and customers gave rise to a suspicion that somewhere beneath her clothing were other, more intimately placed sterling posts, secret points of sensitivity of which she was always slightly, sexily aware. He forked over a five for well whiskey, but she pushed the money back and poured him Makers Mark, a double, and smiled. He thanked her and she said, "What?" and leaned closer so he could speak into her ear. She caught the back of his neck, holding him there, and shouted, "You don't remember me?" He shook his head. "Too bad!" she shouted, and turned to help the next customer.

Some thirty feet away, Pinero was sprawled in an easy chair, the centerpiece of a living room arrangement that included a window seat. He was talking with a group of people, his attitude expansive, at ease. Did they not recognize him?, Dempsey wondered. Maybe the people who drank here were so lost in self-contemplation, they never watched the news. Or maybe Pinero's confidence and affability were sufficient disguise. This might help explain, Dempsey thought, why he himself was recognized everywhere. Part of his mind was occupied in trying to remember the bartender. Her smell of bathwater and soap, the usual female scents, but cooked by the specifics of her metabolism to a mild spiciness—that was familiar. As was the way she moved. Serpentine arms and long-fingered hands that made the acts of pouring, mixing, and clearing seem part of a Balinese ritual. He put her at 24, 25. One of Madison's friends? She was the right age. He still couldn't place her.

Some time later the bartender appeared at his elbow, wearing a green vinyl jacket, and invited him outside, she was on break. He said he was waiting for somebody, but she told him she was only going to get some air and he said okay. They went to stand beneath the awning of the closed Chinese restaurant next door. Rows of darkened storefronts lined both sides of the street. The black air held a polished sheen and due to a complete absence of traffic, the stoplights went red to yellow to green for no purpose, their colors liquefying the asphalt beneath. The freeways rushed and hummed in the distance.

The bartender said, "God, it's like spring! I can't see my breath anymore." She lit the cigarette she'd been holding, exhaled, and smiled at him. They were, he realized, nearly the same height.

"You a friend of Madison's?" Dempsey asked.

"You figured that out, did you? But you don't remember me."

"Okay, this is weird. I think I remember the way you smell."

She tossed her head back and laughed.

Dempsey didn't get it.

"I'm not insulted you don't recognize me. I looked way different. Your basic Catholic college girl. Plaid skirt, demure blouse. Loafers." She cocked her head, assessing him. "You look about the same. A little wear and tear. What happened to your eye?"

He said it was nothing. "So tell me where we met?"

She took another drag, exhaled out the side of her mouth. "About seven years ago. Madison invited a bunch of girls out to the Shore. The fishing cabin?"

"Yeah?"

"You were at law school, home for the weekend. You came down Saturday morning to fish and"—she shot him a coy look—"we liked each other. We went out to the boathouse."

"Yeah... Christ! Marie? Marisa?"

"Marina."

Dempsey had it now and was deeply embarrassed. "Ah, fuck!"

"Almost." She giggled. "We did everything but. I can understand you remembering how I smell."

"My dad," he said. "He drove out to check on things."

"*And* your mom. *And* your uncle."

Dempsey said, "We were..." but Marina kept going.

"The funniest thing was me trying to get dressed in the boathouse and listening to you explaining to your father why he couldn't go in and get his net. You did this whole soliloquy about how you needed to be alone, you had things you wanted to work out, and he kept going, 'It'll just take a second!' finally he's silent for a few and then he goes"—she affected a male voice—"'Okay, but while you're at it, maybe you can figure out where Madison's friend Marina went to.'"

"He can be a major asshole sometimes."

"It was *hilarious*! I mean I wish he'd waited awhile, y'know."

"That would have been good."

Two couples and a single man exited the bar together, walking off in the opposite direction.

"I wanted to call you," Dempsey said.

"Bullshit!!"

"Seriously! I intended to call you. Just when I got back to school, everything went to hell. I ended up dropping out."

"Yeah, you told me you were thinking about becoming a cop. I couldn't imagine anyone wanting to be a cop, so I asked why and you said you just didn't want to be a lawyer anymore."

"I don't want to be a cop anymore, now."

Her face emptied and he presumed she was going to comment on the shooting, offer commiseration; but if that was the case, she let the impulse die.

"I was going to call you, too," she said.

"Why didn't you?"

"Y'know...life." She tossed the cigarette. "I was going to call a few months back. I thought about it when I saw you on TV. But Madison said if I called, you'd catch hell from your girlfriend."

"Not anymore. She bailed."

Marina pursed her lips and remained silent. It was so quiet for a moment that Dempsey could hear the shunting of the stoplight. At last she said, "This person you're waiting for, is she a woman?"

"Not a woman."

"I'm being so uncool here!" She covered her face with a hand. "God!"

"No you're not."

"I *am*!" She half-turned away, plucked a second cigarette from her pack. "Oh, hell!" She turned back. "I had this massive crush on you. When we went to the boathouse I was a virgin. Technically. All the stuff we did, I'd never done most of it. I considered you extremely sophisticated."

"Guess you learned different."

"The experience holds up." She grinned. "I would have saved myself for you, but you didn't call."

He could see them in the boathouse now, rolling around on the bed of canvas they'd made. He remembered how she'd felt, how excited he'd been. Aroused by the ungainliness of her spirit, galloping ahead, then faltering, unsure. They had liked each other and he liked her now. Liked the openness and force of her. If he were to tell Elise what he was thinking, she'd laugh and say something like, Guys! You put a knothole in front of 'em, they'll convince themselves they're in love. But that was the law of Elise's world. Its gravities no longer influenced him. He was between worlds now.

"Want me to call you sometime?" he asked. "I'd like to call you."

She nodded slowly, then vigorously, as if the idea were gaining acceptance. "That'd be nice." She put the cigarette back into the pack. "I should go in, but I'll give you my number."

"It might be better I didn't call right away. I'm going through some bad times. I don't think you want..."

"No! If you call I want you to call soon." She said this sternly, then sighed—a surrender. "Now I'm *really* going to be uncool. I can't believe I'm doing this." She angled her eyes to the side and kept them there as she spoke. "I've thought about you for seven years. Not like obsessively, okay? Just whenever there's a space in my life, I remember Billy Dempsey and I think about giving him a call and seeing where he's at, y'know? I realize you haven't thought about me. Maybe if I was in your shoes, maybe I wouldn't have thought about you. But I believe we were more than a hook-up." She made a bemused noise. "An *almost* hook-up." She turned back to him. "If I'm wrong, I want to find out soon."

"That's what you want." He stared off along the street, listening to the angry rip of a muscle car downshifting. "There's a chance I'm in some danger. The shooting and everything."

Marina jammed her hands into her jacket pockets and studied the pavement. She ran the toe of her tennis shoe along a crack. "I know you're innocent."

"I'm not innocent. I shot the guy."

"You thought you had to."

"Maybe, yeah. But I wasn't...I didn't follow my instincts."

"You fucked up."

"Exactly."

"Because you didn't follow your instincts."

"Uh-huh."

"Well, my advice is..." She gave him a grave look. "Don't do it again."

He laughed, but she didn't join in, just kept looking at him. "Okay," he said. "I see what you're saying. I'll call soon."

"Promise?"

"Absolutely. Can I have a cigarette?"

She stepped close and kissed him lightly, her mouth partway open. "Sure," she said. "For starters."

⅜

PINERO WAS NOWHERE to be found. He wasn't in the bathroom and his chair had been appropriated by a slim animated man with silver hair and a matching soul patch. Berating himself, Dempsey pushed through the crowd to Marina, who was talking to the man on the door, and pulled her back outside.

"Is there a rear entrance?" he asked.

"Yes ... to the parking lot. What's wrong?"

"Shit!" Dempsey threw a frustrated punch at the air. "Shit, shit, shit!"

"What's wrong?"

"The guy I was watching musta gone out that way."

"I thought you were waiting for somebody."

"Waiting ... watching. Whatever." He paced away from her, stood with hands on hips. "Fuck."

"Who was it? I might know him."

"You don't know this guy."

"I might. Most people here are regulars."

He described Pinero.

"That's Tico. You were watching Tico? What for? He's an okay guy."

"You're thinking about somebody different. His name's Pinero. He's not an okay guy."

"Maybe his last name's Pinero, but the man you described is Tico. He comes in every Friday almost. He runs a rave Friday nights. It's probably where he went."

"Can't be the same guy."

"He was sitting up near the window seat with some other people? Drinking Chivas?"

Tico. Runs a rave. It didn't seem possible.

"The rave's in an industrial loft. I can show you."

"Just tell me where it is."

"You'll never find it. Give me a minute."

She hurried back into the bar. He saw her talking to an older woman with strawberry blond hair; she appeared to be pleading her case; she laid a hand on her heart as if making a promise, then came back out. "Let's go," she said happily.

"Look," he said. "If we're going to do this you have to stay away from me once we're there. I don't want him seeing us together."

"Is this like police stuff?"

"It's personal. He's my partner."

"Tico's a cop? He comes over like a player."

"Cops can't be players?"

There was a surge of cheering from within the bar and shortly thereafter two women stumbled out together. Flecks of something white clung to their hair. They stopped on the walkway and shared a deep kiss. When they broke from the kiss they said, "Hi," in unison, almost in harmony, to Marina and strolled away arm in arm. Taped to their backs were placards on which had been handwritten the words, JUST MARRIED.

"Tico was the one who started shooting, wasn't he?" Marina gave her forehead a smack. "God, why didn't I know that? But I still don't get why you're following him."

"Therapy." Dempsey steered her toward his car and when she asked him again, apparently thinking that the answer was a joke, he said, "Matter of life and death."

⋈

THE RAVE WAS HELD on the top floor of a ten-story building situated under the Manhattan Bridge, almost indistinguishable from a dozen other buildings in close proximity, all monstrously gray and anonymous with blank, black windows, like petrified giants whose souls had flown. Dempsey could hear the rave riding up on the freight elevator, heavy-gauge techno rhythms and screaming electronics, and when the door lifted he felt the assault of noise was shifting soft things inside him, compressing and remolding them. The loft was immense, a concrete box long and wide enough to enclose the hull of a naval cruiser, lit by a hazy amber radiance, with a length-of-the-space window that offered a panoramic view of Manhattan. To the right of the elevator, tucked into a corner, was an area sectioned off into an office by white prefab walls—here, Marina told him, was where the private party was hosted. Invitation only. Tico would show up there eventually, if he wasn't there already.

Hundreds of people, maybe a thousand, maybe more, were scattered across the floor. Dancing and twirling glow sticks; attempting shouted conversations; sitting on circular benches arranged about the support pillars. In a pavilion close by the office, under a canvas roof with walls of gauzy cloth, were gathered several dozen mattresses where people lay in shadow, resting, recovering, ODing, making out. Juice and soda were dispensed at a conference table beside the window, draped in a crimson cloth. Suspended from beams above the crowd was an array of banners with psychedelic designs, and upon a high, central, many-leveled platform, the DJs and their intimates gazed down upon the chaos they had made, elevated above the mob like old Stalinist leaders watching the passage of an army on May Day.

Dempsey peeled off from Marina and began to search for Pinero, passing into the throbbing center of the rave, moving along the constantly shifting edges of mini-crowds that formed and dissolved like the cells of a liquid body. For a time he was dogged by a wiry shirtless kid who sought to impress him with his skill at twirling luminescent blue glow sticks, gazing pitiably all the while as if hoping for a treat. Two girls, their faces painted with butterfly designs, tried to drag him into their dance, then a pimply, heavy-breasted girl who couldn't have been older than fifteen, wearing a *Joey Ramone Lives* T-shirt, lurched against him and clung, half-conscious. He lugged her into the restful shadow of the pavilion, lowered her to a mattress, and was about to leave, but noticed two teenage boys hovering like hungry dogs waiting for scraps. Dutifully, he sat with her until another girl—a friend, apparently—fell out beside her and glared at him with hot suspicion. As he stood he caught sight of a thickset man wearing black leather, his slickered hair tied in a ponytail, helping another sluggish, floundering girl to her feet at the edge of the pavilion. He then led her into the office. The opening of the door afforded Dempsey a glimpse of bright red walls and people reclining on pillows. He debated whether or not to stake out the door and decided it would be wise to explore the rest of the loft first. As he moved back out into the crowd, a man with his hair moussed into spikes and bare muscular arms sleeved in barbaric tattoos stared at him with bellicose intensity. On failing to terrify Dempsey, he waggled his pierced tongue and slid away among the jostling bodies.

At one end of the juice table was a slight blond woman clad in a hippie-style granny dress who painted faces for ten dollars. Deciding to augment his disguise, Dempsey took a seat, and, using shouts and sign language, told her to do with him as she wanted. She asked him to remove the patch. He mouthed, No, and leaned back, letting her work. When she finished she handed him a mirror. She had transformed his face into a terrain map, undulant lines of different colors laid over a burnt umber base, describing a system of hills and valleys, the design united around its lowest point, the patch, a black lake at the bottom of a barren land. He wanted to dislike the effect, but had to admit it said something.

People were gathering by the opposite wall, hemming in a large semicircular space. Dempsey saw long chains whirling above their heads, little pots of fire attached to the ends. He shoved his way to the front of this secondary crowd and saw that Marina was the one twirling the chains, dancing with an abandon that brought to mind old Roman Empire flicks, slave girls from Circassia giving their all for the jaded emperor. She dropped to her knees, touching the back of her head to the floor, continuing to keep the ten-foot-long chains whirling, then rose in a single motion to go whirling herself, conveying an alien eroticism, her hips undulating, the length of her arms and legs making it seem she was half snake, half woman, sidewinding through the pounding light. She approached Dempsey, eyes fixed on him with sorcerous intensity, swinging the chains in circles that appeared to cross and re-cross in front of her, the fire pots missing each other by inches, then strutted away, chest thrust out, arms flung back. He was so enthralled by her grace and muscularity that when he felt fingers brush the back of his head, he didn't turn, and the next instant someone ripped his eye patch off and gave him a shove. By the time he righted himself, whoever it was had vanished.

Dempsey fought free of the crowd, looked for someone running, and noticed the floater. As had happened in the bathroom of the Hollywood Lounge, it had expanded, stabilized into a weave of fine black lines that enclosed his visual field. Not the sketch of a corridor, though. It resembled a badly woven net, the web of a drunken spider segmenting the motley shapes and colors of the rave. One segment began to whiten, quickly filling

• 46 •

in; then another segment washed white, and still another, the process gradually whiting out the dancers and the milling crowd. As if he were being walled in with plaster. Before long, only a few roughly hexagonal shapes were left unwhitened, sequentially framing—as he staggered about, his confusion amplified by the tumult—a portion of a woman's face, a section of garishly patterned cloth, and—as he went to his knees, disoriented—a patch of concrete floor. Then he was blind. Wrapped in whiteness; crying out unheard; denial turning to dread. He fell onto his side, rolled over on his back, felt the concrete vibrating with the thunderous, throbbing bass, his ears assailed by an electric ululation like a warped call to prayer. A mosaic of cracks was emerging from the whiteness that encased him, quickly building the image of a black door. Black metal, dull and scarred, with a red knob. Mounted in a white wall.

From this point on the process accelerated. Like a man hurtling downslope on a roller coaster, Dempsey's emotions were compressed into an awful exhilaration. Another mosaic emerged from the blackness of the door, a weave of red lines netting his eyes, and it seemed that he was drawn inside a scarlet enclosure where the music was muffled and something pale and bloody lay upon the floor and a grotesque image stared from the wall. A wooden figure similar to the froglike statue in the botanica, its design more African-looking. More awful in aspect. Then it seemed he was confronting one of its pupil-less mother-of-pearl eyes. Suspended tiny before it, as if he had shrunk or it had grown large—a pale globe that itself bred a third mosaic through which he passed once again into whiteness, though it was nothing like the flat surface that had initially walled him in. This was a luminous pearly volume of space, profound and peaceful and silent, from which was brought forth a final and far more complicated mosaic, a puzzle of a thousand irregular shapes that spread across that depth like pressure cracks across glass, acquiring color, detail and perspective, assembling the image of a world beyond Dempsey's experience and yet familiar, calling to mind the terrain map that had been painted on his face. He was standing atop a promontory, gazing out at a vista of barren hills and valleys, a country of charred colors, browns and blacks blended together. Steep hills linked by spiny ridges; valleys puddled among them; and at the bottom of the deepest valley, ringed by what looked to be monolithic buildings of dirty yellow stone, a hole. An oval of utter absence. A lake, he thought. Surrounded by ruins. But as he watched, the ebony reach of the lake began to roil, to revolve, proving to be a tunnel whose spinning depths were streaked with fire, like the mouth of a sky cave, a wormhole in which galaxies were reduced to cometary passages by the insanity of physics. Whirling pots of fire beneath dark water. Staring at them, he felt movement in his left eye, as if it, too, were prone to such fiery incidents, as if his eye and the thing below were one and the same, or at least correspondent in substance and design, resonant with one another. He glanced up and found that the sky had also evolved into a vortex of fire and emptiness, and recognized that the place were he stood, this bleak topographic model with a hole in its middle, like an architect's simulation of hills and valleys and ruin... this was all the world, a tiny anomaly adrift in an immensity, of no greater significance to the thing enclosing it than the floater in his eye. Casting a shadow. Having that much reality and no more. He waited for cracks to appear in the illusion, for another mosaic to manifest and carry him off. But none came and the thought that he was stranded there, that he was part of the thing he feared, a temporary fixture upon a temporary structure made of earth and rock and the will of god, suspended for some temporary purpose in the humor of Oludamare or some other uncaring idol, dredged a whimper from his throat. He could find no purchase, no point upon which he could balance, no comfort to allay the terror this fantastic yet far-too-personal view of the human condition forced upon him, and he shut down, switched off, like a television picture shrinking to a point of light against a blackened screen, fading if not from that place, then from all awareness of it. ⵜ

H E WAS LYING ON HIS BACK. He could still hear music, but at a remove. A man's voice said, "Here he comes," without enthusiasm, as if merely noting the fact. Hard white light. Dempsey blinked against it. The floater had returned to normal, a trouble in his eye, not a puzzle. And that was good, because everything else was bad. He felt as if he'd been awake for a week, though not sleepy. Wired and freaked. He had too many questions about what had happened to focus on a particular one. He concentrated on the moment.

"Billy?" Marina appeared above him, anxious. "You okay?"

He struggled to sit, but she forced him down. "I'm good," he said, and swung his legs off the cot, touched the floor. A white room with white glassed-in cabinets, like the nurse's office in high school. A beefy man with a heavy beard shadow, wearing an EMS sweatshirt, was standing by the cabinets. "Know what kinda shit you took?" he asked Dempsey.

"I didn't take anything. You got bandages?"

"You musta took something. You's out for almost an hour."

"I got a condition. My eye...light fucks it up." He stared at the man. "I was out for an hour, you didn't call an ambulance?"

"Your vitals were good. Didn't see no point."

"You ever call an ambulance? I mean, working here?"

"No need so far."

"Probably wouldn't be good for business, huh?"

The man shrugged.

"What happened to your patch?" Marina asked.

"Some asshole stole it." To the man Dempsey said, "You got gauze and tape? I need you to bandage my eye."

The man opened one of the cabinet doors. "No problem. But I'm gonna hafta ruin your paint job."

As the man applied the bandages, Dempsey—steadier now, trying to push aside what had happened—said to Marina, "That was some dance you were doing."

"Thank you."

"Where'd you learn to dance like that?"

"I studied with Alvin Ailey."

"You're a professional?"

She smiled. "Just you wait."

Out in the corridor the music was louder, but they could manage conversation and Marina told him Tico had left. "They all came out of the party room a little while after you passed out. Tico went down on the elevator."

Dempsey did not have enough energy to know frustration. "Fuck it. I just wanna go home."

"You look awful." She fiddled with her ear lobe. "Why don't you come home with me. I can fix you some food and you can do the couch thing."

"I should go back to my place."

"I bet your apartment's a wreck and I've got a beautiful couch. Down pillows. A George Foreman fatless grill that makes perfect cheeseburgers." She looked up at him through her eyelashes. "Am I getting a reaction here?"

"I've got some crucial stuff going on. The next twenty-four is real bad. After that, plug George in. I'm there."

"Okay." She drew out the word, giving it a dubious emphasis.

The rave was still tuned to full-on debauch, the music hammering home its brain-deadening point. Drugged children swaying in a breeze only they could feel; bored Jersey girls bummed because they hadn't met any cool guys; nerds wishing they knew how to dance so they could meet the Jersey girls; experienced ravers whose only expertise was rave-ology and had officially critiqued this rave as lame; a Brooklyn Heights dentist who had found out about the place from a teenage patient and hoped by attending to convince his babe date that just because he wore a hairpiece didn't mean he was not young at heart; drug dealers, pimps on recruiting expeditions, likely a predator or two sizing up an intended victim; Friday Night Fever show-offs, lounge rats of the new millennium; a broken-hearted mechanic trying to find his old girlfriend whom he'd heard would be there with her new lover; a couple doing choreographed leaps, in training for *Rave: The Musical*; members of an upstate high school choir down to perform at Saint Patrick's, hoping to score some quality with which to impress their friends back home; dykes, bikers, hackers, slackers, junkies, punks, and who could say, maybe even a monk; at least one kid nicknamed Trips and three girls named Desireé. It was a tired story and Dempsey did his best to ignore the details as he guided Marina toward the elevator. But then he noticed that the door to the party room was black, set in a white wall, with a red doorknob. Like the door in his vision. He went to investigate.

After examining the door Dempsey had no doubt it was the door he had seen. Every scuff and scratch and indentation was the same. What this said about the nature of his experience was problematic, but he felt it went a long way toward discrediting the bits-of-protein theory. Since the only alternative he'd been offered was voodoo, and since all the evidence—admittedly not much—suggested that Sara Pichardo's assessment of the situation was at least not at odds with the truth, he thought it might be helpful to look inside the room. He sent Marina off to mingle with the crowd and tried the door. Locked. He hailed one of the security people, a black man with a laminated ID about his neck, and showed his badge. In a shouted conversation Dempsey told him he wanted to check out the room; the man said he had no key. Dempsey asked him to find someone who did. Shortly thereafter a sweaty barrel-shaped man of early middle age, wearing a black leather jacket, gray slacks, and a ponytail, came walking up and handed over a business card. Robert Borghese. Black Sun Productions. He had a scornful, pompous air and resembled the man who earlier had led a drugged girl from the pavilion into the office. Dempsey conveyed to him that he suspected narcotics use in the room. Borghese mentioned something about a search warrant. Sure thing, Dempsey said. He pulled out his cell phone and by means of shouts and pantomine informed Borghese that he would call for the warrant, some back-up. Once his colleagues arrived they would check IDs, do strip searches, and like that. Understand? Borghese didn't care for the prospect and two minutes later Dempsey was alone in the room.

Closing the door cut the music by half; the comparative silence made him feel more stable. Red walls, a cheap oriental carpet, and pillows of various colors strewn about. A stand mounted on the rear wall, just the right size for holding statues with pale bulging eyes. The most curious thing about the room was the strong scent of a cleaning agent. It wasn't likely that a group of people partying at a rave would be so responsible as to tidy up. Dempsey rolled back the carpet and found beneath it an oval section of damp concrete some ten feet long and six feet wide. A tingly something broke loose from his spine and took up residence between his shoulderblades. He recalled his apparent passage through the room, the impression he'd had of a pale, bloody form lying on the floor. He inspected the floor and the bottom of the carpet. No visible blood. He kicked the pillows around, searching for spatters. On the underside of a pale blue pillow he spotted a dark stain. A splotch not much bigger than a dime. Still tacky. With a penknife he cut away a swatch of cloth bearing the stain. Lacking an evidence bag, he tucked it into his wallet.

The memory of Borghese—if it had been him—leading a less than fully aware girl into the office; the stain, the damp floor; the similarities between the things Dempsey thought he had seen and what he was seeing now: it would have been easy to make a leap of judgment and conclude there had been a blood ritual in the room. But there was no absolute connection, nothing he could depend on. One thing offered an ounce of validation. The statue into whose eye he had seemed to pass had been similar yet not identical to the one that had drawn his attention at the botanica. If all he was experiencing was a result of mental problems, a self-punishment arising from paranoia and guilt—and he couldn't dismiss the possibility—then the likelihood was that he would have worked an identical statue into his delusion, not one with subtle differences in design. Something bad is happening, Sara Pichardo had told him. Feel where you are in the world. Think about what happened and what will happen. Well, where he was in the world was lost and as for thinking, analysis was off the board. All he could do was connect the dots, but when he did no definable shape emerged and he was not in a position to wait for one to emerge. He was due to meet Sara Pichardo at the church in twenty-one hours. Partial shapes and hints. Instinct. These would have to guide him.

He wanted to retreat, to return to his apartment and take pills. Drink vodka. Turn on the TV, cut the sound, put on something mellow. Lucky Dube or the Congos. Watch Clint Eastwood Versus Godzilla. But either he had lost his appetite for these consolations or else he no longer trusted in them. He reconsidered Marina's invitation. He wanted to feel secure and she was offering security, comfort, real concern. Things he needed. He opened the door, spotted Borghese lurking and beckoned. Once Borghese was inside, the door closed behind him, Dempsey pointed to the damp concrete and said, "You have an accident?"

"Shit happens." Borghese's eyes darted about the room.

"Question is, was it legal shit—" Dempsey beamed, "—or that other kind?"

"What're you talking? There's nothing illegal here. Just pillows and a fucking rug."

"And a big damp stain. Let's not forget that."

Borghese had a hunted look. "Somebody musta puked."

"They were very neat. They rolled the carpet up first. Top of the carpet's not wet. Go on…give it a feel."

"I'll take your word."

"Maybe I should ask Pinero. I bet he could help me out? You know Pinero, right? Tico?"

"I got an idea. Why don't you gimme your name, your badge number." Borghese pulled a notebook from his jacket, unclipped a pen from his shirt pocket.

"Somebody tell you I'm a cop?" Dempsey gave him a wide-eyed stare.

"You're not a cop." Borghese shifted his feet, adopting a more aggressive pose. "You better hope you a fucking cop!"

Dempsey drew his pistol, angling it loosely toward Borghese. "I got a gun. That work for you?"

Borghese eased back a step, held up his hands. "Hey…fuck!"

"Looks like a cop gun, don'tcha think? I mean somebody came up to me with this here and said they were a cop, I'd say, 'Hey, that's cool.' That what you'd say?"

Borghese worked at presenting an impassive face.

"Tell me, Bob. I saw you haul a girl in here. Little fifteen, sixteen year old girl. What happened to her?"

"Look, the girls wanta come. After that…y'know. Whatever."

"More precise, Bob. What happens to the girls?"

"What do you want, a fucking fairy tale? You know how it is."

Dempsey repeated the question and Borghese, looking as if might be ready to consider desperate measures, said, "Sex things, I guess. I don't hang around."

"Sex things," said Dempsey musingly. "I guess."

He caught Borghese by the shirt collar, jammed the gun barrel under his throat, and ran him back against the wall. "Me and Pinero one time, we were interrogating some guy and I did a whacko cop act to loosen him up. Pinero said it was fucking Oscar-worthy. He said the reason I played whacko cop so good's 'cause I was a little whacko myself, y'know? I didn't agree. I thought I was in complete control. But lately I been wondering if he didn't nail it. Things have been not going well. No voices in my head. Nothing like that. Just shit all the time. It's like I can't get the cap screwed back on the bottle. You ever feel that way, Bob? Like you can't get the threads right and your stuff's fizzing out?"

A flicker of something, a light dawning, surfaced for a moment in Borghese's face, and Dempsey said, "Uh-oh! Know what you did there? That little twitch behind the eyes. Down at the cophouse we call that 'the old giveaway.' You know who I am, don'tcha? You figured it out."

Speaking between gritted teeth, Borghese said, "I don't know shit about you!"

"I know the old giveaway when I see it, Bob. You figured it out. Which means you're tight with Pinero. And if you're tight with Pinero, you're Scum-of-the-Month Club material. Which means I don't fucking care what happens to you." Dempsey pulled back the hammer. "Know what I really hate? I hate guys who make little girls disappear."

A change came over Borghese. Suddenly he was calm. "You're not going to shoot me."

"What's this, Bob? The Power of Positive Thinking?"

Borghese maintained his poise.

"You think I won't risk it? 'Cause of witnesses? Fuck! You could butcher a whale out there, nobody'd notice." Dempsey pushed the muzzle into Borghese's larynx. "I got away with whacking the PR. You think I won't get away with whacking your guinea ass?"

Borghese stood mute, but there were cracks in his armor.

Dempsey screwed the barrel a millimeter deeper into Borghese's flesh. "It's not like I'm debating moral issues here. I need a reason not to do this and I just can't think of one."

"It's some kinda religion thing," Borghese said. "I don't know what they do with the girls. It ain't good, I know that. I seen blood in here, I seen all kindsa shit. But what the fuck's it about, I don't know. I just do what he says."

"Pinero?'

"Fucker owns me, man! He owns me, my company... everything."

"Black Sun Productions? Pinero owns it?"

"He owns everything."

"I need more." Dempsey tapped the barrel against Borghese's forehead. "Tell me who I can talk to."

"None of those guys'll talk. They're stone, man. They're scary fucking people." Borghese made a throat-clearing noise. "Maybe this girl useta work for me. Pinero was fucking her. After she got with him she came to me for money. She was dead frightened of the guy. She moved, she changed her name. Maybe she'll give you something."

"You know where she is?"

"Yeah, I send her money. She owns me, too."

Dempsey picked up Borghese's notebook and pen, tossed them over. "Write it down."

Borghese wrote, then handed him the notebook. Dempsey glanced at it. Donna Kass. The address was in Staten Island. "This woman's dead frightened, all she does is move to Staten Island?"

"She gotta sick kid lives with her ex." Borghese dropped his chin to his chest and breathed heavily. "She didn't want to move away too far."

Dempsey pocketed the notebook. He trained his gun at Borghese, intending to use it as an educational aid, but as he steadied the barrel he had the impulse to fire. He felt stainless, freed of accountability. He thought he could sense a red echo of what had happened in the room. This man had enabled it. This fat fuck Tony Soprano wanna-be with a wedding band embedded in the flesh of his ring finger who each night went home to a duplex sty in Jersey where his skinny pig children stole from his wallet and his overstuffed pig wife would imitate pleasure and grunt beneath him and the next day he would sally forth in his fucking fully loaded Olds with garnets on the mud flaps spelling out Kiss Me I'm Sicilian and sit in his office grope his secretaries and make phone calls to other fat fucks with whom he colluded to defraud even less powerful fat fucks and then once a week served as acolyte in a church where his sole duty was to deliver young girls to men who did sex things I guess and turned them into damp spots on a concrete floor...

"Hey! Don't!" said Borghese, wetting his lips. "No shit! I told you all I got, man."

Dempsey had to break free—it was as if the air had hardened into stone and was holding his arm in place. He angled the barrel away from Borghese. "We had a moment just now," he said. "Know what I'm talking about?"

"Yeah."

"And you know what I've been going through lately, right?"

"I read the papers."

"That's good. Then you probably got a read on how close to the edge I'm walking."

Borghese nodded and licked his lips again; his eyes avoided Dempsey's.

"Take it to heart," Dempsey said. "Tell your friends."

⅜

PEONIA TEA TASTED LIKE LIQUEfiED DIRT, but Dempsey drank every drop and crawled beneath the covers that Marina had arranged on the couch. He'd expected her apartment to be thrown-away furniture, bad metal sculpture, coffee cups used as catch-alls, old band posters. But Marina was a girlie girl. Fluffy pillows; well-tended plants; sunny yellow paint with white trim; women's magazines on the coffee table; several framed dance programs; baskets of cachet emitting a perfume of natural ingredients. No cute pictures of kittens in view, but a casual search would probably unearth one.

She came out of the bathroom in a T-shirt and baggy shorts and turned off the overhead. The moony glow of a streetlight came through a window behind the couch, making shadows from a forked branch of the maple out front. She sat on the edge of the couch, asked if he had everything he needed, told him where to find the coffee and said not to worry about waking her in the morning, she'd go back to sleep. He knew she wanted him to touch her and he took her hand. She rubbed the back of his knuckles with the ball of her thumb.

"How's your eye?" she asked.

"It's been bothering the hell outa me, but I'm not feeling it now."

"My soothing influence. It never fails."

"Think that's it?"

"Oh, yes. I have that effect." She interlocked her fingers with his and said in a cautious tone, as if it were something she wasn't sure how to say, "I hope I'm not alarming you. I know I came on pretty strong."

"Do I look alarmed?"

"You did at first. You still seem a little reticent." She shifted and her hip pressed against his. "I guess that's Tico and everything."

"That's all it is, believe me."

"Okay." She gave his shoulder a quick buff with her free hand. "I won't ask any more questions now, but I . . . Will you tell me what's going on eventually?"

"Sure. How 'bout Sunday morning? We'll go for coffee."

She nodded solemnly and sat looking past him toward the window, then, leaning down, kissed him with her cool lips and minty tongue. He wanted to pull her close, but she slipped away, leaving him a whispered, "Good night," her padding footsteps and the click of the bedroom door. The maple shadow quivered on his blanket; a spray of ice chips pattered against the pane. The warmth of her hip had faded, but he still felt connected to her.

He tried to organize his Saturday. Drop the bloody swatch of cloth at the lab. Interview Donna Kass. Dig up more background on Israel Lara. That was the part he couldn't put together—where Lara fit into this. Were he, his relatives, or his fairy godmother responsible for the floater? Even if he was not, knowing more about him might point to whoever was responsible. And if, as Dempsey was starting to believe, Lara's death had been an execution, what reason would Pinero have to arrange it? Then there was Sara Pichardo. Why? How come? Whither?

Figuring all that out shouldn't take more than a week or two.

He turned his face to the cushions, recalling a conversation with the shrink about why he slept with his face covered, and then pictured Marina in her bed. How strange it was that whenever things were going to shit, something good happened along and made you feel even shittier because you were too messed up to cope. For a while he'd been on a streak of dating women who looked stable until you got close enough to see the bats circling. In reaction to this he had taken up with Elise, whose idea of a healthy relationship was so thoroughly standardized—marry, breed, accumulate, die—he would have welcomed a bat or two. From Marina, though, he had a feeling of strength based on a bright consistency of spirit. According to his splintered memories of the day they went to the boathouse, she seemed the same forthright, energetic soul she had been then. He wanted to come to a conclusion about her, to be certain of her in some way. Just to have one certainty. But if conclusions were possible, he was too tired to reach them. His thoughts fractured into pictures, urges, and he fell asleep thinking how she had looked walking toward the sofa, her upper body in shadow, long legs gleaming in the milky light.

)(

LYING ON THE COUCH the next morning, face smothered beneath a pillow, he felt the floater trembling in his eye. The sensation made him nauseous and he wanted to dig a knuckle into the humor, crush the thing into submission. He fumbled for his patch, couldn't find it, and swung his legs onto the floor. The cold light was a numbing agent, the maple branch an extraterrestrial ulna with two digits of black bone attached. Stiff-legged, squinting, he went into the bathroom, splashed his face with water and turned on the shower. Above the toilet was a framed photograph of a kitten. Waiting for the water to run hot, he returned to the living room and looked out the window. The view was a portrait of entropy. Gray air, gray sidewalk, gray snow. An ancient gray-haired woman bundled in a gray coat, leaning on a cane, inched along between rows of apartment buildings with blank reflectionless windows, like the disapproving faces of gigantic maiden aunts hidden behind thick spectacles. Just watching her made Dempsey feel decrepit.

He opened his left eye to see how the floater was doing. The area surrounding the tangle of cell-like structures was swarmed by elusive manifestations that variously resembled the souls of jellyfish and pubic hairs encased in gel. It was getting to be a fucking Disney cartoon in there. Ectoplasm Central. He closed the eye and glanced down at the street again. A thick-bodied white guy in baggy jeans and a hooded Jets coat had fallen in behind the old woman. Though he could have easily passed her at a normal pace, he was keeping about ten feet behind and doing your basic perp scan, scoping out the street, checking doorways on either side. Dempsey raised the window and spat noisily. The white guy looked up and Dempsey shook his head with deliberate slowness. He stood guard at the window until the guy, walking fast, rounded the corner, and the old woman, trembling with the effort, began mounting the steps of her building. Dempsey's heart seemed to tremble with the same awful inconstancy, to fill with a ghostly contagion.

He stood under the shower with his head down, hands braced against the tiles, until he fit his skin better, and then soaped himself, whistling under his breath. The floater continued to vex him, but the water was a distraction. He considered the day ahead. Chances were he would have to frighten Donna Kass. Use Pinero to scare her worse than she was already scared... The shower curtain divided, his heart jumped, and Marina slipped in beside him, she went to tiptoes and took a peck at his lips. Turning, she plucked a pink round soap with scalloped edges from the dish. On the swell of her right hip, sloping down onto her buttock, was a tattoo—a skinny black oblong, irregular in shape, with squiggly lines around it. Seven of them. Dempsey wanted to touch it. He flattened his palm against the tattoo, molded the curve of her waist, and slid his fingers around to touch the underside of her breast.

"Oh good!" she said. "I didn't want to wait anymore."

They made love with Marina's back to the wall. The picture of the kitten rattled. Her right leg hooked behind his knee, her hands were clasped at the small of his back, and he imagined himself entwined by a slippery female vine that writhed around him in constant delicate motion. Her eyes rolled up so only the bottom of each iris was visible, beautiful zombie girl. Breath sang out of her, blending with the rush of the shower, making it seem the water had a voice. He loved being inside her, plugged into her sinuous energy, her white voltage, with her nails nicking his skin, the devotions of her wordless whispers almost speaking the things her body told him. He loved how she arched when she came, an arc completed, jolted into a cry, and he also loved how she accommodated his spasms, his clutching, when he came seconds later, gentling him down, easing him back into the real. She clung to him afterward, suddenly sleepy and murmurous. The water hissed around them, cascading from their bodies onto the porcelain. Dempsey felt washed so clean, he worried that the city air might kill him.

♓

PINERO'S EX-GIRLFRIEND, Donna Kass, rented a third-floor walk-up on Westervelt Avenue in Staten Island, part of a neighborhood known as Georgetown. Westervelt transected a hill a few blocks up from the ferry landing and was a street where Dempsey himself had lived for several months while studying law at Columbia. The buildings were decaying brick Jefferson townhouses with gray wooden porches and wrought-iron fences and concrete front yards, some having square unpaved areas that permitted the survival of an elm, an oak or a maple, trees planted during the neighborhood's prime eighty years before. In Dempsey's day he had frequently found people smoking crack on the landings of his building, and walking out in the mornings he would crunch dozens of empty crack vials underfoot; they might have been the product of a kind of weather that recurred each night, a glassine hail spat from a violent cloud. The porch steps had been littered with rubbish: busted toys; wine bottles wrapped in the soaked remnants of brown paper sacks; condoms; scraps of food; lumber and bricks for some half-assed home improvement that would never see completion. Vivisected motorcycles rusting in the yards, their chrome skeletons trapped in a mire of ripped lawn furniture, broken glass and plastic, cellophane wrappers, soiled articles of clothing, all flattened and compressed into a weird matte that counterfeited a lawn. The street had appeared to be evolving into a mutated wilderness with day-glo leaves, mechanical bushes, flowers of pure spoilage. At some point during the intervening years the area had been cleaned up. The drug dealers who had patrolled the streets, crying out plaintively beneath their customers' windows, were gone, as were the schizophrenics—homeless whackos exported from Manhattan on late night ferries by the cops—who had wandered about talking in loud voices to whatever agency they believed controlled the secret mechanisms of the universe, their routes and hours of appearance as regular as those of pilgrims performing a circumambulation; but the houses remained in a state of profound decay and disrepair, huddled together like elderly beggars along a curb, and Dempsey knew it was only a matter of time before the drugs and the crazies and the rest of the garbage blew back in and reclaimed the neighborhood.

Donna Kass, who admitted Dempsey after a lengthy delay, was slender, tiny, and large-breasted, pale as an onion, her eyes a watery blue and her hair coppery red and unkempt, hanging in strings to her shoulders. Her voice carried a touch of rural twang and she had one of those smooth childlike Appalachian faces that seem genderless and not quite formed, empty of experience, reminiscent of the saintly, spaced-out children who often occupy the backdrops in medieval depictions of the Passion. That unfinished look in contrast to her voluptuousness caused her to seem much younger than her thirty-two years. At casual glance she might have been taken for a well-endowed fifteen-year-old, and perhaps, Dempsey thought, it was this quality that had appealed to Pinero. If Borghese was sending her money, she spent hardly any of it on interior decoration. They talked in a dingy, high-ceilinged room that was furnished with a TV, wooden chairs, a broken exercise bicycle, a table covered with newspapers and unopened mail, and a sprung sofa bespotted with dozens of cigarette burns. The walls were cream-colored, water-stained, and the fireplace crammed with empty pizza boxes and paper sacks from a Chinese take-out joint, these the apparent source of a sour stench. Donna had no visible tracks, but given her dazed anxiety and the furtive air of her male friend, who clattered off down the stairs less than a minute after Dempsey's arrival, a high probability existed that Borghese's money was going straight into her bloodstream.

Wearing a house dress beneath a stained Jets T-shirt, Donna sat on the sofa, knees together, chain-smoking. Dempsey moved one of the wooden chairs so he could sit facing her. When he asked about Pinero she appeared stunned and then said with flustered defiance, "I don't care what kind of papers you wave around, I ain't talking about him." She took a drag on her cigarette, but didn't draw the smoke deeply, exhaling a cloud. "Why you wanna know about him anyway?"

"Detective Pinero's the subject of an investigation. If you have information concerning any illegal acts he may have perpetrated, this would be a good time to reveal it."

"Illegal acts!" Donna's disdainful snort suggested that she found the term inadequate. "How'd you find out about me? It was Bobby Borghese, wasn't it? That son-of-a-bitch!" She flopped back against the cushion, put a hand to her forehead. "Aw, man!" She collected herself, and butted her cigarette in a clamshell ashtray. "I ain't talking about Pinero."

"Would it surprise you if I said we suspect Pinero of murdering a young girl?"

She turned her head slightly away and touched the hair along the nape of her neck. She remained silent, but nothing in her manner indicated surprise.

"Things are going to come out now," Dempsey said. "The quicker we take down Pinero, better it's gonna be for anyone with a reason to be afraid of him."

No reaction.

"The longer he's on the street, the more he's likely to learn about the investigation. He might start trying to clear up loose ends."

At this her level of alertness elevated a notch and she lit another cigarette.

"I hear you got a kid," Dempsey said. "Pinero know about him?"

She flashed him a bitter glance. "Keep your mouth off my kid!"

"It's not my mouth's your problem. People are gonna be talking to Pinero. He'll learn what's going on."

Holding the cigarette in two fingers, she rubbed the inside of her right wrist furiously with the heel of her left hand; her eyes roamed the room. "Did that fat bastard Borghese tell you about me? Say!"

"I spoke to him."

"Jesus Lord! Once Bobby goes to yapping…Shit!" She hung her head, shook it slowly back and forth as if dismayed by the sight of her knees. "Okay, I'll tell you some stuff. But I ain't gonna testify to any of it and soon as we done I'm outa here." Her chin quivered. "You better not let him walk on this."

"We don't let anybody walk on a homicide."

Donna's eyes teared, but she managed a laugh. "Aw, hell no! You already let him walk on the one!"

Dempsey's face may have betrayed a comical degree of confusion, because she laughed again and said, "Don't you know even? The one on TV. The Puerto Rican guy. Lara."

"You believe Lara was a homicide?"

"Never was no mention on the TV about Pinero knowing the guy, was there? Kinda makes you think."

"Pinero knew Lara?"

A caginess came into Donna's expression. "I ain't saying another word 'less you give me money to travel on. Today! I need it today."

"I got maybe sixty bucks."

"I need a thousand. No…fifteen hundred. And don't tell me about department policy, how it takes time and shit. You got a bank account. You wanna hear 'bout Pinero, you can pay me yourself!"

Dempsey tinkered with the idea. "I'll take you to an ATM. I'll give you what I can. But first you tell me something about Lara and Pinero. After that I'll drive you wherever you want and you can tell me the rest."

After a pause she said, "If you're fucking me over, man…" She flicked cigarette ash in the direction of the ashtray. "I saw 'em twice together. Once we were staying at a hotel in midtown. The Penta. Pinero knew the manager and he got us a suite. I was sleeping and I heard someone talking. They were in the living room. The door had fell open a crack and I saw Lara."

"What were they talking about?"

"I can't remember much. One thing they kept coming back to was 'the black sun.' They wasn't saying '*a* black sun,' it was '*the* black sun.' It sounded weird, y'know. Frst off I thought they's talking about a man. A black son…a boy child. But they kept saying '*It's* coming,' '*It'll* be here 'fore we can be ready.' Things like that."

"What's that mean? 'The black sun.'"

"All I know's they were revved up about it was coming in a few years. Like they had something important to do when it came. I don't know what. I was sleepy, I didn't listen long. But the 'black sun' thing, it was weird. It stuck with me."

"When was this…when you heard this?"

"A few years back. End of 'ninety-nine." Donna stubbed out her cigarette. "The other time's a couple years later when I was living on West Seventy-fourth. I was expecting him, but he was late…"

"You were expecting Pinero?"

"Mm-hmm. I was getting worried 'cause it was after midnight, so I peeked through the drapes to see if he was coming. Him and Lara were outside on the street, arguing."

"You could hear them?"

"Nah, you could see they was shouting, though. And Pinero gave Lara a shove. Near knocked him down. Lara had something in his hand. A little sack, maybe. He threw whatever was in it onto Pinero. He was making funny gestures, waving his hand in circles, and Pinero was brushing off stuff from his jacket." The stubbed cigarette was still smoldering and she ground it out. "I closed the drapes, so I can't say what happened after that. But Pinero was in a shit mood, so it wasn't, y'know... it wasn't about nothing."

"Did Pinero know you saw him with Lara? Either time?"

"No way! He wouldn't tolerate me messing with his business. If he thought I was, he woulda gotten on me."

"Then why are you afraid? Why would he want to hurt you?"

"That's what you gonna pay me for. Don't worry, it's worth it. I got proof." She stood, smoothed out her skirt, and stepped toward the rear of the apartment. "I'm gonna throw some clothes in a bag and wash up."

While she busied herself in the bedroom, Dempsey thought about how Pinero had suckered him and Haley, about Black Sun Productions and the black sun conversation between Pinero and Lara. About what had happened in the bathroom at the Hollywood Lounge, at the rave, and about what Sara Pichardo had said: "You know something bad is happening..." Yes he did. He knew it now. Voodoo. Conspiracy. The very real possibility of murder, of sex crimes. Yet some ounce of insane rationality inside him refused to accept the validity of what he knew. The floater gave rise to doubts—he wanted to deny what he suspected of its nature and so he looked for doubt. But doubt was becoming difficult to sustain.

Pipes rattled as Donna ran water in the bathroom. A car passed on the street, its tires grating on the icy pavement. It was the first sound Dempsey had noticed from outside since his arrival. He recalled how noisy the neighborhood had been when he lived there. Boombox racket, disputes escalating to curses and shrieks, the occasional gunshot. It was as if that tide had withdrawn, leaving behind the shabbiness it had created, and no new tide had come in its stead. As if the law of the place was: The absence of evil is the only good.

He hauled out his cell phone, thinking he would check with the lab and see if they'd finished the blood work on the scrap of cloth, but realized it was too early. He began poking around the room. The letters on the table were all junk mail and bills. Credit cards, electric, cable, one from a storage facility. Several were marked Final Notice. Beneath the bills lay a crinkled square of tin foil that held traces of brownish white powder. Dempsey didn't bother to inspect it closely. He glanced into the bedroom. Clothes on the floor. A scarred chestnut dresser; an unmade bed with a cloth overnight bag atop it. The sheets bore what he took for a subtle gray design of clouds, but that proved to be grime. Taped above the bed was a detailed charcoal study of Donna, showing her in a tank top, holding a sketch pad on her lap. It had the stiff feel of a student self-portrait. She had made several changes in herself. Enlarged her eyes, sharpened and strengthened her nose, added smile lines at the corners of her mouth. The effect was grotesque, like a face drawn on a doll.

Dempsey listened to the running water—Donna was filling the tub. He called out, "You taking a bath? I'm in a hurry here!"

"Hold your horses! I be out in a minute!"

Irritated, Dempsey returned to the living room and sat on the sofa, a position that allowed him to watch the bathroom door. He fixed his mind on what he had learned from Donna. Lara and Pinero involved in some arcane complicity relating to "the black sun." Which a few years ago they believed was due in a few years; which might mean that now was the time of its advent. Then a falling-out between them. Then the shooting at Lara's apartment. It was the skeleton of motive, but in order to flesh it out he had to learn more about "the black sun." About Black Sun Productions. He should have squeezed Borghese harder. Chances were slim that he'd be able to track him down today. He checked his watch. Fifteen minutes had elapsed since he'd spoken to Donna. He walked over to the bathroom door and said, "I've got appointments! Let's go!"

No reply.

He put an ear to the door, heard nothing, but smelled a pungent herbal scent. "Miz Kass!"

More nothing. Dempsey's scrotum tightened.

"Donna?" He pounded. "Hey! What're you doing?"

He thought he could hear a faucet dripping.

"I'm coming in!" He tried the door.

Locked.

"Fuck!" He kicked the door, splintering the wood around the lock. He kicked again. The door slammed open, its bottom hinge ripped away. Moist heat boiled out around him. The tub, an immense clawfooted model, was brimful of murky brown water; eel-like weeds clotted the surface, clumped into bright green islands. Donna was gone. Her dress, panties, and T-shirt lay atop the clothes hamper. Afraid that she might have changed clothes and gone out the window, he peered through the paint-stippled glass. There was a three-story drop and no fire escape. He looked to the weed-choked surface of the bath, spooked by the thought that she was hidden beneath it. He pushed back the sleeve of his jacket, groped for her hair and pulled her head clear. Her eyes were open, one iris partly rolled-up. She wasn't breathing. He wrangled her out of the tub, slopping water and weeds across the tiles. A rubbery arm encircled his waist as he waltzed her around. He laid her down on the tiles, tipped back her head and tried mouth-to-mouth. When he started to hyperventilate he quit trying but stayed kneeling beside her, rattled by the sorryness of death and the sad, smoky taste of her mouth. He shrugged off his waterlogged jacket and forced himself to examine the body. Tracks on the inner thighs. None fresh. He turned her over. On the right buttock was a tattoo of an elongated black oval, slightly lopsided, with squiggly lines radiating from it.

Identical to the tattoo on Marina's hip.

As he turned Donna again, fluid leaked from her vagina onto his fingers. He washed his hands at the sink, resisting the urge to puke. Still queasy, he opened the window, sucked in cold air. He glanced at the body. Donna's coppery hair had spilled across her face. One arm was draped across her abdomen, her hand covering her genitalia as if in demure reflex. Her pink skin glistened. Weeds decorated her lolling breasts.

Steadier, but disconcerted by the connection between Marina and Donna, Dempsey went back into the bedroom and dumped the contents of Donna's bag onto the clouded sheets. From her wallet he removed ID, a photograph of a scrawny red-headed boy eight or nine years old, a baggie containing what he estimated to be a week's supply of heroin even for somebody with a major league habit. In a coin purse he found two keys, one with a stamped number and an enameled logo that was familiar. He sifted through the mail on the living room table—the logo on the key was the same as the logo on the bill from the storage facility. He pocketed it and continued his search, but as he pawed through panties and bras, skin creams, hair brushes, Hershey Kisses, cosmetics, crossword magazines, all the relics of Donna's woefully unexamined life, the baffling circumstances of her death eroded the methodical cop program into which he had lapsed and he began to feel unfocused, spiritually enfeebled. He sat on the edge of the bed for a couple of minutes, regrouping, then returned to the bathroom. The herbal aroma had degenerated to a reek; weeds slimed the floor. He eased around the body and ran water from the tub faucet into his cupped palm. Clear. Not brown. He rummaged through the medicine cabinet, the shelves underneath the sink, working from an assumption that Donna had added something to the water, some new age herbal concoction to treat the skin. Aspirin, mercurochrome, empty valium bottles, dental floss, toothpaste, cleaning agents. Using the coffee cup in which she kept her toothbrush, he scooped up some bathwater. Particulate fragments were suspended in it. He touched his tongue to the water. The taste was a bitter counterpart of the reek. Logic told him that she had drawn a bath of untainted water and then something had been poured into it. He must, he thought, be missing something. He explored beneath the tub, behind the toilet, in the clothes hamper. He searched the bedroom again, hoping to unearth an empty container, a plastic jug with a label reading Swamp Weed Beauty Soup or some such. Unsuccessful in this, he kneeled beside the body and checked the scalp for contusions, for a sign that she might have struck her head and knocked herself out. No lumps, no contusions. Given her emotional state, he doubted she would have fallen asleep, certainly not deeply enough to drown. Suicide was a possibility, but drowning yourself was a hard ride, especially if you had enough heroin to produce a quick OD.

A nagging inner voice clamored for Dempsey's attention, an abrasive, insistent voice haranguing him for refusing to admit the obvious, saying you know something bad is happening, some voodoo shit went down in here, she was lying in the bath and something materialized in the room, some figment of a curse, some shadow thing, and it scragged her, because that's the only explanation for the stink and the geechee water in the tub and a dead woman who had drowned without a struggle. The voice raged on and on, unmindful of the fact that its audience was desperately trying to tune in an assuring CNN-type voice issuing from the control cabin of his brain, carefully explaining that there was no need to panic, what now appeared incomprehensible would eventually prove to be nothing out of the ordinary, and they would simply fly over this spot of bother and before he knew it the fasten-your-seatbelt sign would be switched off. A crawly feeling edged along the back of his neck. He was tempted to look behind him, but was afraid he might discover that the roof had been lifted soundlessly away and an enormous brutal face with pale blank eyes was peering in, taking note of the policeman and the woman whom he was kneeling beside, as unreal from that perspective as the figures in a dollhouse tragedy, and what a mess they were in, the woman's soul wandering, searching for a strong womb in which to be reborn, and the policeman with his prints all over a potential crime scene and a murdering partner who had involved him in something that might be worse than murder. Stressed and despairing, Dempsey had a moment in which it seemed possible to retreat from everything, to shut down and remain kneeling at Donna Kass's side until led away by blue-coated arms. But then he was joined in his vigil by a new presence in the room. It seemed that a great beast had laid down next to him, displacing a volume of air and giving off a heated vibration. The impression was so palpable, he scrambled to his feet in fright, slipping on the wet tiles, staggering back against the door, and caught sight of the tub. The weeds floating in the brown water were drifting together, being urged into eight groupings, slithering across the surface as if tugged by invisible fingers, gradually shaping a message. There were two separate rows. Four letters on top, four on the bottom. The first letters to become legible were H E L, these the initial three in the top row. The last letter on the bottom row proved to be a Y. Transfixed, Dempsey waited until four more of the weedy letters could be read and the message spelled out:

H E L   O

B I   L Y

Then, less afraid than outfaced by the situation, incapable of putting it into a frame, he ran from the apartment, pelted down the stairs and out onto the porch steps, gazing along the deserted street, trying to recall where he had left the car, marked in this by an ugly brindled dog that stood stiff-legged on the sidewalk beyond the iron gate and seemed in its dazed and trembling fixity to be every inch Dempsey's familiar.

)(

AFTER RETRIEVING THE CONTENTS of Donna's storage unit—a single suitcase, almost empty—from a facility on Victory Boulevard, Dempsey drove to the parking lot of the Staten Island ferry, where he sat watching a ferry approach, trying to order his thoughts. The ferry disgorged fifty or sixty passengers, mostly women with kids, who headed for their cars or began walking up the hill into the moribund neighborhood he had recently fled. Once they had dispersed he rested the suitcase on the seat next to him and pried off the locks. Inside were a sketchpad and a large wooden jewelry box containing a dozen or so expensive-looking pieces. Tucked into the sketchpad was an 11 by 14 manila envelope that held a sheaf of photographs. The subject of all the photographs was a room with red walls very like the room where the private party had been held during the rave: pillows strewn about; the carpet rolled back. Painted or chalked on the uncarpeted concrete floor was the design of an elongated black oval surrounded by seven squiggly lines. In each of the photographs a different young girl lay naked at the center of the oval. In some of them a man—different men— was having sex with a girl; in the rest, the man stood half-clothed, as if preparing to have sex, conversing with other men who sat upon the pillows. In one of these latter, the girl at the center of the oval was Marina. She looked almost as young as the day he had met her at his father's fishing cabin. She sported no tattoos on her arms—only the one on her hip. The man getting ready to have sex with her was Pinero. Among the onlookers was Israel Lara.

Dempsey tossed the photographs onto the seat and stared off toward the dock. Under the dead sky the ferry was pulling out again, and he felt that he was pulling out along with it, sailing away from the situation at the same steady pace. He rested his head on the steering wheel. A stretch of blank time seemed to be spliced into the stream of his day. After a while, heavy with disappointment, he once again took up the photographs and shuffled through them. He recognized no one else. In the sketchpad were a number of charcoal portraits. Nine men. Two of the men portrayed also turned up in several of the photographs. Frustration surged through Dempsey and he slammed the heel of his hand against the wheel and said, "Fuck! Fuck!" He resisted the impulse to have a second look at the photograph of Marina. There was no need. Every grainy millimeter was imprinted on his memory.

The ferry had drawn far enough away that it resembled a red toy boat propelled by a miniature wake, pointed toward a forbidding, bristling island. Without the World Trade Towers, the skyline looked strangely neutered, and Dempsey found himself speculating as to how long it would take before this view seemed normal. He switched on the ignition, let the engine idle. Because he could think of nothing else to do, he decided to meet Marina after her dance class. Whatever else she might be, she was part of the problem now.

His cell phone rang. He punched Talk and said, "Dempsey."

"*Hola, macho,*" Pinero said. "What's going on?"

"You tell me."

Pinero chuckled. "Who can say? These are strange days, eh?"

"What do you want?"

"Just wondering how long it's gonna be before me and my partner get back to fighting crime."

Dempsey picked up the photograph of Pinero and Marina and Lara. "I got your ass, man."

"What's that?"

"I said I got your ass."

"My ass? Hang on. Lemme check." Then: "No way! I still got my ass. Must be somebody else's ass you got."

"I got a picture of you and Lara together."

"Damn! I thought the little fucker looked familiar. Guess I musta forgot."

"I'm gonna find a Kinkos and mail copies to people who'll fucking love 'em."

"Double jeopardy, Billy. Worst can happen they'll file conspiracy charges. Then you'll be going down with me. I gotta feeling it won't come to that, but we should probably get together. You free tonight?"

Dempsey heard a touch of laughter in Pinero's voice. "I talked to Donna Kass."

"Donna...wow! Did you fuck her? She got this sexy *Deliverance* thing happening. How's she doing? Last I saw she was going down for the third time." Pinero chuckled. "Drugs, y'know. Bitch is always floating on something."

"What're you trying to say?"

"Don't sweat the small stuff, Billy. Time's too short. Hey, you still wearing the patch? Take that bad boy off. Have a look around. You missing half the world. A new and better day is dawning."

After Pinero hung up Dempsey sat recalling the last couple of times he had removed the patch; but he realized that he had to know. He flipped up the patch and stared across the water and waited for the lines to appear. No lines manifested. Instead, the cell-like structures in his left eye began to contract, swiftly aligning into a simple shape that—once complete—seemed to live not within his eye but to be an immense object on the horizon, half-obscured by the skyline: a lopsided black oval with lesser squiggly shapes radiating from it, rising slowly above Manhattan, its outlines bulging and indenting like a mutant sun being extruded under inconceivable pressure, squeezed up into the ashen winter sky from a world of darkness below.

⧲

NOT FAR FROM THE DANCE STUDIO, near the corner of 34th and Lexington, was a yuppie coffee bar with little oval-shaped black tables and a chattering, cheerful, good-looking crowd of businessmen and secretaries, and the windows all steamy, hiding the smoking traffic that clogged the streets and pedestrians hurrying along with their collars up and heads down like frightened refugees and the crusts of blackened snow on the curbs. Marina led Dempsey to a table against the back wall. She was red-cheeked from the cold, wearing a white wool cap, a turtleneck, jeans. She warmed her hands over a cappuccino. Watching her, Dempsey wanted to pretend that he had not seen the photograph and Donna's tattoo. He wanted to have a trivial conversation, to be at ease with her. But when she glanced up from her cup and smiled at him, he said, "I just came from the apartment of a woman who has the same tattoo you do . . . the one on your hip. Her's was a little lower on her butt."

The smile flickered. "Her butt, huh? Should I be jealous?"

"Nothing to be jealous about. She was dead."

He didn't believe she was faking her startled reaction. "She had some photographs," he said. "You're in one of 'em. Lying on a concrete floor. On a painted design that looks like the model for your tattoo. You're about to have sex with Pinero."

She rested her head in her hand, shielding her eyes from him.

"It was taken in the private room at the rave," he said.

"I know."

"There's guys sitting on pillows and watching."

Angrily she said, "I know!"

"Wanta tell me about it?"

"No, I don't. You want to tell me about your sex life the last seven years? I'm sorry you had to see it, but it's not relevant anymore."

"Not relevant to what?"

"To me!" Her voice grew more strident. "Didn't you go through a phase when all you wanted to do was fuck? Haven't you fucked people you wish you hadn't?"

The couple at the adjoining table—a nerdy twenty-something man in a ski sweater and a well-tailored woman perhaps ten years older—gazed at Marina with interest.

"Do you want me to explain my behavior?" she asked. "Will that make you happy?"

"Look, I just..."

"I don't mind. I'm not ashamed. I went a little wild when I hit the city. I did drugs, I was promiscuous."

The woman at the next table had stopped paying attention, but the nerdy guy was fascinated.

"Tico had great dope. Two hits and you just didn't care. He kind of talked me into doing it, the time in the photograph. But it was my decision." She removed the wool cap and shook out her hair. "I had a fling, but I'm different now. God, I haven't had a boyfriend in almost a year!"

Put on the defensive himself, Dempsey said, "This isn't about me being judgmental."

"Oh, no?" She leaned back. adopting a cynical expression. "You have health concerns, maybe?"

"Okay. It fucked me up. I wasn't expecting to see something like that."

She waited for him to go on.

"But it's not just about that. It's this whole thing with Pinero."

The anger came back. "The thing you're investigating? You think I'm involved?"

"Not involved. But you might have information that'll help me."

"I don't see how."

"Let me ask you some questions without you getting pissed. All right?"

After a few beats she said, "Go ahead."

"The tattoo. How did it come about, you getting it?"

She let out a huffy sigh. "If I tell you about it, you owe me one. You have to forgive me sometime when I screw up, because this is definitely a screw-up on your part. I don't deserve to be interrogated."

"It's not an interrogation."

"It's not chit-chat, either!" She folded her hands about her cup. "Pinero was always flirting with me, telling me how hot I was, talking sexy. Kidding around. I knew he was only half-kidding, but it was no big deal. He started telling me about this weird club he was in. Black Sun. How they initiated a different girl every weekend. He told me all about it over the course of... I can't remember how long it was exactly. Months. He said the girls all liked it. They got a free tattoo, great dope. I kept telling him it wasn't for me. But then I broke up with this guy I'd really liked and I started drinking and drugging. One night I said what the hell. It was like I was being defiant. Defiant against what... I don't know. Fate. God. Maybe myself. Maybe I just hated myself. That's what my therapist said. Anyway, Pinero took me to this place out in Green Point and I got the tattoo. We went to the rave and he got me high. I was totally wasted."

"It might have been treated... the dope."

"Whatever... maybe. I was so stoned I got off on guys watching me. I felt incredibly sexual. Earth-motherish. Later I didn't feel so good about it, but at the time it's like it was all happening in some special context."

"Do you remember what else was going on in the room?"

"It's pretty fuzzy. There were drums. Drumming. Not from the rave. Inside the room. It must have been recorded. I didn't see anyone with a drum."

A waitress bearing a tray upon which were heaped nuggets of an orangish breadlike substance hovered and asked if they cared to sample "our new pumpkin biscotti."

"That's okay," Dempsey said. "Thanks."

As the waitress moved off, Marina said, "There was a statue on the wall. It looked African."

"Did you know Lara was in the room?"

"The guy you sh...?" She broke off, looking contrite.

"That's right. The guy I shot. He's sitting on a pillow."

"He was in the room? Are you sure?"

"I can show you the picture."

"No," she said coldly. "Thanks for offering."

"Actually I'd like to show it to you. See if you can identify any of the men."

She had a sip of cappuccino. "I think you better tell me what's going on."

"It'll sound crazy."

"I won't let you treat me like a suspect. If you want me to do something I'm not eager to do, you have to explain why it's important."

The waitress with the pumpkin biscotti was at a nearby table. Dempsey signaled her, brushed off the free sample again, and asked for an Americano. As he told Marina what he had gone through and his thoughts concerning it, he came to believe the story implied by the events he described, as if saying it confirmed his suspicions, proving an underlying logic he had not known existed. He came as well to believe that Marina's involvement with Pinero was not significant. All her reactions were unforced, completely natural. He hadn't allowed himself to indulge in suspicions before picking her up at the studio, but now he felt the weight of that potential for worry leaving him.

It took him two coffees to get through his recital. When he

finished he popped the chunk of biscotti that the waitress had pushed on him with the second coffee into his mouth, chewed, and said, "These people need to rethink their biscotti strategy." He swallowed and wiped his mouth. "Sounds crazy, huh?"

"Maybe. But... I don't know. Do you believe it?"

"So many pieces lying around, there has to be a puzzle. Your tattoo and Donna's, the thing you were lying on... it's the black sun. It's gotta be. Fuck that is, I don't have a clue. Maybe I'll find out tonight. Right now I need you to take a look at these pictures." He pulled the manila envelope from his windbreaker and handed it to her. "If you recognize someone I might be able to talk with them."

Reluctantly, she opened the envelope. Her mouth thinned as she examined the photographs, studying each thoroughly before proceeding to the next. "Some of them look familiar, but I can't be sure." She came to her photograph and peered closely at it. "God, it is Lara." Her eyes flicked up to Dempsey. "Can't you use these against Pinero?"

"Not without fucking myself."

He filled her in on his phone call with Pinero.

"You should at least make copies," she said.

She started going through the remainder of the photographs. She picked one up, studied it closely. "Carrie!" she said in amazement. "My God!"

"Carrie?"

"Carrie Lang. She was a friend of mine."

He took the photograph from her. Carrie Lang was pretty, a blue streak in her black hair, some babyfat on her hips. Blissed out; her eyes closed. A fat hairy-chested man wearing chains and an amulet was nailing her from behind. His head was down, preventing a positive ID, but it could have been Robert Borghese.

"She disappeared about four years ago... No, five years," Marina said. "They never found her."

"Where was she reported missing? Brooklyn?"

"She lived in Chelsea, so it must have been Manhattan. Why?"

"Pinero worked in Missing Persons five years ago."

"You think he handled the case? Can you find out?"

"I could look into it, but five years ago... If there was anything to learn, it's probably gone by now."

Sirens sounded outside; no one apart from Dempsey bothered to look up from their coffee and conversation. Through the steamy glass he saw fire trucks moving toward a disaster farther downtown.

"At the rave," he said. "The wet mark under the carpet? I figured they'd cleaned up blood, because of the spatter on the pillow. I thought Pinero must be slaughtering women in there. Sacrificing them. Then I learned you and Donna Kass had survived the experience and I decided I was wrong. The wet mark's gotta be where they washed off the design of the black sun. Now I don't know what's going on. Maybe he's killing some of the women."

"I never felt in danger."

"Well, you wouldn't have, right? The great dope and all." He drained the last of his second coffee. "I don't think any of this shit matters. It's all coming down tonight."

He leaned back, let his eyes rove. Everyone in the place was sitting at a table that resembled a little black sun, and he had a spasm of paranoia, the thought that these sales reps and secretaries and marketers and Internet specialists were actually adherents of a religion that worshipped an evil plasma body, and now he had stumbled among them and they were every one laughing at his confusion, anticipating his fate. He told Marina he had to go. She caught his arm and said, "I know someone who might be helpful."

"It's almost noon," he said. "I got things to do."

"You're not going to figure this out in ten hours. All you're doing is following a trail of breadcrumbs."

"That's how it works. Cops don't lock themselves in the study and play the violin till they get the big insight."

"But you have no idea what's going on! You're not even sure if this is something you should be afraid of, and this..."

"I think I got that much straight."

"This guy I know might be able give you some perspective."

Dempsey relented. "Who is he?"

"One of my professors at the New School. Don't look all Oh-God-a-professor-they-don't-know-jack-about-the-real-world! Randy writes books on the subject. He's kind of an asshole, but he knows his stuff."

"What're you talking about?"

She interlaced her fingers with his and affected a mysterious look. "Voodoo!"

)(

RANDY—PROFESSOR Randolph K. Heckler—was a stubby little man with a big-beaked gnomic face that seemed to be peeking through the salt-and-pepper bush of his curly hair and untrimmed beard with an expression of dazed inquiry. He wore jeans, a work shirt, and a leather sport coat. Something resembling a small Tiki doll dangled on a string about his neck. His office had the tacky ambiance of a Florida souvenir shop, walls decorated with objects of wood, coconut shell, feathers, and bone, and also with framed photographs depicting a younger, thinner, be-sandaled Randy in various tropical climes, a number of carved and painted hand drums suspended in clusters, and several scraps of paper, also framed, upon which were inscribed—in red, black, and green chalk—samples of a curious iconography. Atop his desk a computer and a waterless fishbowl containing a plastic castle and a solitary turtle were menaced by unstable towers of books and papers. When he saw Marina in his doorway he said, "Hey, Spooky. Where you been?" On seeing Dempsey he did a double-take and said nothing. And after Dempsey, at Marina's prompting, told his story, Randy asked her, "Is he for real?"

Dempsey stood and said, "Thanks for your time."

"Don't take it personally. You come in selling a story like that, it's not out of bounds for me to question your credibility."

Marina leaned toward him across his desk. "For God's sake, he's a cop. He's not going to be making something like this up."

"Ordinarily I'd agree with you. Cops aren't blessed with much imagination. But I read the papers. Officer Dempsey's imagination is in terrific shape."

"That's 'Detective'," said Dempsey, and then, to Marina, "Let's go. I don't need this shit."

"Just hold on." Randy kicked back in his chair, rested his feet on what appeared to be a camel saddle. "It's a hell of a story, *Detective*. Got some interesting elements. What do you want from me?"

"I told you!" Marina said. "We want you to help us understand what's going on."

"As to the *voudon* aspects, correct?"

"Randy calls voodoo *voudon* because he's such an expert," Marina said with thick sarcasm.

"It sounds cooler." Randy crossed his legs, cradled the back of his head in both hands, a posture that caused his beer belly to protrude. "What's going on is fairly evident. You've gotten yourself in the middle of a power struggle between a santeria temple and a group of Shango Baptists. The most interesting thing is the material concerning the black sun. I've never heard of an instance in which the ritual was actually performed."

"You know about the black sun?" Dempsey sat back down.

"Oh, yeah. It's an old *voudon* legend. I assumed it was only a legend, but now..." He reached out a finger and turned on his computer. "Every once in a while—infrequently—there comes a day when one of the gods becomes vulnerable. He can be displaced. Oludamare, the supreme being, and all the rest, they don't get called out. But Olukun, the warrior figure. He has to cope with a challenge."

"Who challenges him?" Marina.

"The black sun is a proto-god. A god-in-waiting, if you will. It provides the challenge by possessing a man it deems worthy and then doing battle with another man possessed by Olukun. It's purported to be different from ordinary possessions in that the god doesn't completely take over the one possessed.

It's more like a hitchhiker dozing in the passenger seat. He's there to help if his champion gets into trouble." Randy tapped a key and the sound of a dial-up modem was heard. "If Olukun wins, nothing changes. The black sun slips away into oblivion. If the black sun wins, it becomes Olukun. A new aspect of the god. I've read texts that refer to the new aspect as potentially more violent and erratic." Randy typed in a command. "The challenger and the god fight as men in the world of men. But since the black sun is the challenger and Olukun, due to his eminence, is considered the stronger, the world they fight in's the one that would exist if the black sun were victorious." Randy grinned. "Sort of like home court advantage in the play-offs. Of course the challenger is also Olukun, albeit a variant form of the god. He's likely no weaker than the old god, just less experienced."

More at sea than ever, Dempsey felt a kinship with the turtle, who was trying to mount the toy castle that ruled his world.

"It's an extremely cool legend. Very sophisticated. Jungian stuff. Ah!" Randy spun the monitor around so they could see the screen. The screen displayed an article and heading the article was the image of the black sun. "This what you saw? The tattoo...the design on the floor?"

Marina said, "Yes."

Dempsey said, "I don't get how this relates to me."

"All I can do is hypothesize," Randy said. "But what you've told me suggests that Pinero and Lara were devoted to bringing about the black sun's challenge. They had a falling out. They probably both wanted to be the horse that carried the black sun. The one that would be possessed. Pinero won the struggle and Lara went looking for the support of a temple so he could get back at Pinero. The fact that he sought out Sara Pichardo may indicate he wanted to become Olukun's horse. I don't believe Sara was forthcoming with you. From her reaction, I'd say she thinks you're Lara's replacement. She sent you on a quest for knowledge. That's standard practice in these matters."

"What do you mean 'standard practice'?" Dempsey asked. "You said the black sun was...it rarely happened."

"Infrequently. I said 'infrequently.' Like once every decade or so. If it happens at all. But there are a number of other reasons why someone might be specially prepared to carry a sacred rider." Randy swung the monitor back around and typed. "All this is metaphorical, of course. The conflict between the Baptists and Lukumi Babalu Aye demands a metaphor to make it seem more significant than it is. So they've chosen to view it as a cosmic battle. That's how the prevailing wisdom would interpret things, anyway."

"Is that what you think?" Marina asked.

"What you're basically asking is whether I believe *voudon* works. Obviously it works on some levels. It's successful as a religion, for one. It scratches that itch for a great many people. I've been witness to cures, to a number of things I can't explain. So I'd have to say it also works on a deep psychological level in certain instances. Either the power of suggestion is vastly underestimated, or else *voudon* is for real. But the pantheon...it's hard to swallow. *Voudon*'s a syncretic religion developed by slaves. A pound of Nigerian animism, a pint of Christian mysticism. It doesn't seem reasonable that its basic tenets would be other than a form of accommodation. Then again, gods are metaphors for incomprehensible forces. Maybe those forces don't care they're swapped around and called by various names." He turned his attention to Dempsey. "Let me ask a couple of questions, Detective. After the shooting, after Lara was down, did you come near the body?"

"Yeah. Me and Haley both. We checked to see if he was alive."

"Was he?"

"Barely."

"Did he speak?"

"He tried. I couldn't make out what he was saying."

"And when did the problems with your eye begin?"

"Before the trial sometime."

"So several months after the shooting?"

"About. Yeah."

Kicking back in his chair again, Randy talked to the ceiling, twirling his right forefinger for emphasis. "The logic of your story is compelling. It may be bullshit. Maybe you stepped into the middle of a power struggle and now you're using it to construct a justification for what happened to Lara. People are adept at warping reality in the service of denial. But most stories I hear, you can't hang a theory on them. They're too eccentric. Yours, I can fit a theory to, no problem. It holds together." He cocked an eye at them. "You know why Pinero wanted Lara dead?"

"They had a falling out," said Marina.

"That's what precipitated the shooting, but it's not the motive. Let's say Lara and Pinero engage in a struggle for primacy within their church. After Pinero wins, Lara goes to Sara Pichardo. The support of a strong *mambo* is essential to someone who's going to carry a god into battle. He still wants the job and he doesn't care which god he carries. Or perhaps he does. Perhaps he's lost faith in the black sun. Perhaps he's seen through to something he doesn't like. Certainly he wants to avenge himself against Pinero. Now Pinero, though he bested Lara in political infighting, he sees him as a dangerous host for Olukun. He'd rather fight someone who's not so well-prepared. So he kills Lara." He twirled his forefinger in Dempsey's direction. "A practitioner of *voudon* would say you became involved because at the moment of his death, having no other choice, Lara passed something to you. Perhaps to you *and* the other detective. Detective Haley. I'm talking about Lara's charge, his connection to Olukun. Pinero's happy now. His opponent will be someone who's not prepared. Someone who doesn't even believe in what's about to happen."

Dempsey made a disparaging noise.

Randy stared at him without expression.

"It's bullshit!" said Dempsey. "Possession? Come on!"

"If you think it's bullshit, why are you here?"

"Suppose Billy doesn't show up at the church?" Marina asked. "Wouldn't he be safe then?"

"If he runs he better run far, far away. Pinero will come after him if the detective here's in reach. Pinero sounds like a true believer. He believes implicitly. He feels he has a profound connection with the black sun. That may explain why he engages in sexual ritual. The gods of *voudon* have their attributes. Baron Samedi enjoys gifts of cigars and rum. Erzulie is fond of mother-of-pearl and the color blue. The black sun may be into blood and sex." Randy did his finger-twirling thing and pointed at Dempsey. "Bullshit or not, you don't show up at the church, Pinero still needs an opponent. If it's not going to be you, he'll try to kill you and transfer the charge to someone else who he thinks is weak. If he succeeds Olukun will turn his eye on that someone else."

"You should leave town now!" Marina put a hand on Dempsey's arm.

"Pinero may not be your thorniest problem," Randy said. "Sara volunteered to help you. That tells me she believes Olukun finds you acceptable. She'll want to keep you here, too. I imagine she's aware of your movements."

Dempsey, partly to distract himself, partly because the turtle was staring at him, tapped sharply on the side of the fishbowl. "You said this was a power struggle. What sort of power struggle?"

"In Brazil, where *candomble* is widely practiced, where the church has a public face, it functions like a mainstream religion. Priests and priestesses on TV. Open ceremonies. But most places *voudon* churches are different from mainstream churches. For one thing, they don't proselytize. To a degree, they still consider themselves a secret society. It's a hangover from slavery days when they had to practice their rituals in secret. If you want in, you come to them. Because of this they have a limited growth potential, and if one church starts gaining too much power, drawing adherents away from the rest, you get a power struggle.

I imagine the black sun has been drawing people away from the other New York churches. Sara Pichardo would probably tell you that's because the black sun is coming." He chuckled. "Be a trip if she's right."

Lifting its head with what seemed pugnacious intent, the turtle crawled toward Dempsey's finger. "So what should I do?" he asked.

"You have to go with your feeling on this one, Detective. But it seems you're boxed in. You have evidence that'll hurt Pinero, but you can't use it because it'll hurt you. You have other, less solid evidence that suggests you're being watched. So it may do you no good to run. Your other option is to utilize Sara Pichardo's help. She can give you her strength though the ritual." Randy sat up straight and rested his elbows on the desk. "I can't advise you, but if you choose door number three, I'll bring a drum and come along with you tonight."

"How's that gonna help?"

"I'm a practitioner myself. I've churched at Lukumi Babalu. My drumming'll give you extra energy. Trust me on that. This is all about energy."

Dempsey glanced to Marina, who was fiddling with the bindings of one of Randy's books, and then back to Randy. "I thought you didn't believe in this crap."

"I never said that."

"You said it was hard to swallow."

"I said some of it was. Of all the people who walk through the doors of Saint John's or Saint Patrick's, how many do you think buy every fragment of doctrine? Some buy hardly any of it. But something works for them. They pray, they tell the rosary, they go to confession. They strive for faith. That's how it is with me."

"You're just curious, Randy," said Marina. "You want to see what happens tonight."

"Sure I'm curious. That's my goddamn job description. But I wouldn't involve myself if I wasn't serious. This is as serious as *voudon* gets."

Dempsey said, "I can't get my head around this."

"I will give you one piece of advice," Randy said. "You've got enough facts to make a judgment. But if you're considering going to the church, you need to stop running around the city and calm yourself. The calmer you are, the more successfully you'll carry the god."

"I'm calm."

"Not calm enough." Randy swiveled about to face Marina. "Are you guys an item?"

"Item-ish," she said.

Randy swiveled toward Dempsey, performing the maneuver with a touch of zest, like a kid trying out his dad's big chair. "I was you I'd let this beautiful child of Yemanja take me home and soothe me. Kick back for a few. Get your head clear."

"Child of Yemanja...?" Dempsey had too much information; he decided he didn't want to know.

"Ask her," said Randy. "She took my course."

"Comparative religion." Marina lowered her head, fitted the white wool cap to her hair, and patted it into place. "It was required."

♓

DEMPSEY FELL DEEP into Marina's bed, deep beneath the down quilt, tangling in the cool sheets, foundering among pillows, driftily watching her move atop him, Burmese idol slim and pale with her wide heartbreak mouth and dancer's muscles rippling in her thighs, his pleasure building with dreamlike slowness, as if pleasure were a bath in which he was submerging without the least demanding thought, until he drowned in a soft glowing sensation and was suspended for a while. At last he bobbed to the surface. Marina collapsed beside him, pulling the quilt over their heads, entombing them in a dark cozy warmth, silent except for their breath. She pressed herself against him, her heartbeat telling time against his arm. Dempsey felt ensorceled, under instruction not to speak until she moved. She made a faint noise in her throat, shifted, and he said, "Hey." She shushed him, snuggled closer. Seconds passed before she said, "Sometimes I have trouble talking after."

"You wanna sleep?"

"Mm-hmm."

He slipped from beneath the covers, pulled on his briefs.

"Where you going?" she asked weakly.

"Living room."

"Are you all right?"

"I feel great." He stepped into his trousers. "Must be all that child of Yemanja stuff."

Her eyes closed. "Don't let me sleep more than twenty minutes, okay."

He kissed her, picked up his shirt, and went into the kitchen, opened a bottle of water and drank greedily. In the living room he sat on the arm of the couch, buttoning his shirt, gazing out the window at the pewter sky. He could still smell Marina's skin. Some kids ran past below the window and their shrieks seemed to be an expression of the knifelike gray sections of glass into which the maple branch divided the panes. He crossed the room and stood looking down at the street. On the corner, three bangers in baggy blue athletic gear were throwing half-speed karate kicks at one another. Whenever a passing car slowed, the shortest of them would show himself to the driver, lift his shirt, rub his belly.

Got smack.

Two bare-legged hookers in dyed winter furs, mauve and electric green, wobbled across the icy street, as unsteady as parrots on a broken perch. The corner boys beckoned; the hookers spoke together; the two parties merged; money and drugs changed hands. Mauve and Electric Green tottered off to dreamsville. The corner boys mock-humped the air behind them. All like a brief chapter in a novel nobody would ever want to read. Sometimes Dempsey's father talked about the old days in New York. Fun City. The high society mayor John Whatshisname. If you believed the folks who lived in Manhattan or yuppie Brooklyn, New York was becoming Fun City for real. Midtown a theme park, a tackier-than-Vegas collection of Hard Rock Cafés and the like. And maybe that was the future. Fun City everywhere. Franchised reality. But Dempsey believed there was more evil in the world than ever before. It had just been hidden behind the doors of the corporate board rooms and swept into corners. Every year on his vacation he went down to Honduras, a true geographical corner. An unnoticed, unimportant place. Every year he found the country more riddled with violent crime, with sex tourism and AIDS, with drugs and with street terror, with the malfeasance of development banks, and the backwash of that tide, which had flowed down from the north, was now washing onto the American shore. 9/11 had directed people's thoughts toward a distant menace, taken their minds off the shadow next door. Maybe it was the Republicans or maybe the will of God. Maybe just the way of the world. Whatever the cause, evil was dressing slick, walking tall, and handing out business cards at cocktail parties, and if you didn't believe it, ask the people who lived in East New York, in Georgetown, in Fort Washington. Ask the detectives who worked sex crimes. Ask the corner boys. Whatever portion of evil the black sun promised, in Dempsey's mind it couldn't be much worse than what was already in plain view.

He turned away from the window and began snooping about, examining book jackets, scoping out the framed dance programs, made happy by finding Marina's name thereon. It was strange how at ease he felt. Whenever his thoughts turned to Pinero, Sara Pichardo, all the rest of it, the subject seemed to slide away, its surface too slick to provide mental footing. He could detect no fear in himself and he wondered if this meant that he had come to a decision of which, for the moment, he remained unaware. He had no intention of running. Where, after all, would he go? Jersey wasn't far enough and far, far away wasn't an option. He lay down on the couch, leafed through a woman's magazine. Amazing, the things you could do with those cardboard tubes inside rolls of toilet paper. Spanish lace was making a comeback for June brides. He read half an article entitled "Nine Ways to Exercise Your Love Muscle." Number Four sounded as if it might hurt. He heard a phone ringing and recognized his cell—hanging in the closet, his jacket pocket. He caught it on the third ring and said, "Yeah, Dempsey."

"Phil Paoli, man. I gotta get home. You want your results?"

"Aw, shit! Yeah. Sorry, man. I forgot."

"You forgot? I busted my ass getting these today."

"I owe you, okay? What you got?"

"Mostly nothing you wouldn't expect. Ecstasy and grass, probably ingested at the rave. Methamphetamine taken maybe twelve hours previous. One weird thing. A herb...peonia."

Dempsey tried to fit this fact with all the rest.

"You hear me?" Paoli asked.

"Yeah."

"It's an anti-spasmodic."

"I know what it is."

"She was loaded with it. She musta chewed the whole goddamn bush."

"We talking about a fatal dose?"

"Nah! But she was majorly relaxed."

"Yeah, I think I know the feeling. Okay, man. Thanks. I owe you."

"You run up a helluva tab already. I was a bartender, I'da cut you off at Christmas."

"You'll get your reward in heaven, Phil."

"I'm counting on it."

Dempsey tossed his phone onto the couch and returned to the window. The corner boys were still happening. New friends slowing, stopping to chat. The idea that he might be working behind a massive dose of peonia, that this was the reason for his lack of anxiety, troubled him, but not so much that he cared to do anything about it.

Marina padded into the room, dressed in panties and a maroon Angelika sweatshirt, holding a glass of apple juice. "Did someone call?"

"It was for me. My cell."

She settled on the couch, tucked her legs beneath her, and studied him. "I like making love with you."

"Honest? I couldn't tell."

She threatened to throw the magazine he'd discarded at him.

"Me, too," he said. "It was beautiful."

"Beautiful." She said it as if she didn't understand the word.

"Yeah, it was like...easy. Like I didn't think about any of the clinical shit. It was just all there."

She had a couple of sips of juice. "I guess that qualifies as beautiful."

"I'm not saying it right."

She straightened her legs, curled her toes. "Maybe it's my memory, but didn't you used to be more articulate? You said some lovely things to me out in the boathouse."

"Probably I been hanging out with cops too long." He sat on the arm of the couch, caressed one of her feet.

She had another sip and set the glass on an end table. "I thought it was beautiful, too. I'm just being cautious."

"You think I'm gonna hurt you?"

"I don't want to care about you more than you care about me. I need to be cautious. Anyway"—she set her glass on the end table—"it's way too early to be having this conversation. I'm just taking the temperature."

"There's an article on that in your magazine there. 'Taking Your Man's Love Temperature'."

"Wow! You didn't even flinch when you said 'love'."

"I doubt I'll be doing much flinching around you."

"You think?" She flung herself toward him, coming to her knees and springing forward, hands clawed; she looked disappointed when he failed to react.

"You scared me, honest," Dempsey said. "It's just when I'm tired like this, my reflexes are slow."

"That's good. I want you to be a little scared."

The bubble of intimacy that had enclosed them earlier reformed and for a moment it didn't seem possible to speak. Marina drew up her legs, rested her chin on her knees, saying, "I'm going to make myself a grilled bacon, cheese and tomato. Would you like one?"

"Awesome."

"Would you like two?"

"Two would be better."

She drained her juice and rose from the couch in a graceful unfolding and headed for the kitchen. Dempsey watched the street for another minute, but when he saw an argument developing between the corner boys and a passenger in a black

SUV, he followed Marina and stood behind her while she fried bacon, his hands on her waist. She rubbed her butt against him playfully and told him to sit down or she'd burn herself. He took a chair at a breakfast table of unfinished wood. The clock over the stove was one of those that emit animal noises on the hour; it had kittens instead of numerals and a speaker grille on the bottom. Marina started talking about her class, about an audition that was coming up, a dance version of Aristophanes's *The Clouds*. Immersed in the simmering, ticking warmth of the room, Dempsey responded in monosyllables, adding a downbeat here and there, looking at her legs. He liked that she said "made love" when referring to their encounters. Elise had usually said "have sex" or "fuck" or—when in a sentimental mood—"sleep with," expressing a kind of ideological defiance, as if this would prove her modernity, her maturity.

Marina brought the sandwiches and milk. In the face of her expressed need for caution, Dempsey had an urge to say something incautious and instead of reining himself in, as would have been typical, he said, "Know what knocks me out about you? This force I saw in you when you were dancing. It like stepped right out of you."

She pushed a fragment of tomato around on her plate with her thumb. "What do you think it was...what you saw?"

"I don't know. Just something wanted to make itself known."

"It's weird we have to talk," she said after an interval. "If we were quiet right now, I think we'd know more. People always have to talk, they have to proclaim things. And it's good...it makes me feel good you saying that about me. Maybe it's even necessary. But it's like talking, you have to think about what's said, and you lose contact with the other person a little."

"You always analyze this much? What a bummer!"

Half a smile surfaced. "I remember what I liked about you first thing. You have the nicest way of teasing me. I hate being teased, but I don't mind when you do it."

"Now who's proclaiming?"

"Me, I guess. See what I mean?"

She trailed the tips of her fingers across his knuckles. Five pitiful meows—warped, digitally unhinged—issued from the clock. They both glanced up at it, a self-conscious acknowledgment, as if needing a break from one another.

"I guess I'm going to the church tonight," Dempsey said. "I'm not leaving New York and I'm not blowing the whistle on Pinero. I don't want to go through another trial. Five months, man. It just sucked. The lawyers, the fucking media. I'm not doing it again."

"If I was with you, that might make it easier."

He took firmer grasp of her hand. "I don't have much faith in *santeria*, but what could it hurt? I'll still have the option."

"You know Pinero's going to try to kill you."

"Well, I'm not real clear on that. I'm in a room, he's in another room somewhere, and we're going to kill each other? That's the deal? Maybe that'll work. If it does, if that's what happens"—he wiped his mouth, crumpled the napkin—"then okay. I didn't like killing Lara. I never wanted to kill anybody. But I can do this. Pinero's not so much. He's nobody I can't kill."

Dempsey's bones heavied as if newly burdened. It seemed that an ashy residue of what he'd said put a roughness in his voice. "It's not like a macho thing...a cop thing. It's just I'm to the point, y'know."

He tried to read her face, emotions flickering and then gone, like fish in a fast-flowing stream. He could feel the push of her anxiety, though, and knew that anxiety was, for now, the stream in which her thoughts were flashing.

"It's too dangerous," she said faintly, caressing his arm, studying her fingers as they moved, as if she were creating an effect. "You should go."

He had a desire to confess, to tell her things he'd done as a cop, how Pinero had mindfucked him, made him believe that these things were necessary, how it had changed him, and that maybe he needed to come back at Pinero, maybe it was the only way he could get clear of the past; but blaming Pinero for everything was too facile and he didn't want to delve into the matter of his own responsibility. He put a hand on the back of Marina's neck and pulled her close. His heart felt light and easy. "I should stay," he said.

$$\text{H}$$

SANDWICHED BETWEEN a ninety-nine cent store and a corner grocery on 165th Street, its windows blacked out and its yellow plaster facade embellished with arabesques of blue, red and brown, the Church of Lukumi Babalu Aye resembled a low-rent titty bar more than a place in which forces were being marshaled to decide the fate of a voodoo god and thus the city, the world, and—if you were to credit the basic underlying assumption—the fundamental make-up of the universe. Several businesses on the block remained open, and despite the cold, men were loitering on the sidewalk in front of them, leaning against cars and standing beneath awnings, smoking and talking in islands of light, teasing two shopgirls who arm-in-arm were running this gauntlet, all presenting an image of village amiability; but two blocks farther along, among the projects, crumbling lion-colored cliffs sixteen stories tall, each with dozens of broken windows—there none of the streetlights functioned and no traffic passed, pedestrian or otherwise, and the dark end of the avenue appeared to run straight out into oblivion. Looking off along it, Dempsey had the feeling that something was resisting his eye, withholding necessary visual information, as if a subtle force were counterfeiting a view, blinding him to a significant shape or movement.

A stooped elderly black man, tiny as a child, clad in white trousers and an ancient suit coat open to expose his bony chest, greeted Dempsey and Marina at the door of the church, speaking in English so whispery and disjointed they could not understand what he wanted of them until he took Dempsey by the arm and guided them into a large room at the rear of the building. The walls were whitewashed, as were the floor and ceiling, these surfaces decorated with hundreds of symbols similar to those inscribed on the scraps of parchment in Randy's office. Iconographic figures drawn in red, green, and black, some no more complicated than hen tracks. It appeared they had stepped inside a package that had been somehow inverted, so that the giftwrapping—white paper imprinted with an arcane design— now faced inward. About fifty folding chairs were arranged along the walls, nearly half occupied by Hispanic men and women sitting in small groups. The women—mostly heavy and middle-aged—had on white dresses, and the men wore *guayaberas* and dark slacks. They displayed more than casual interest in Dempsey, casting sharp glances his way and whispering. Several men sat on the floor in a corner, holding hand drums between their knees. Randy was among them. He acknowledged Marina and Dempsey with a wave; the middle three fingers of both his hands were taped together. At the center of the room stood a long table covered in a red cloth, and pedestaled upon it, surrounded by plates of chicken and rice, slices of orange and mango, melons and pineapples, piles of red flowers—hibiscus, bougainvillea, carnations—was the pale-eyed wooden statue Dempsey had seen in the botanica. A strong smell of spoilage issued from the table and as he passed it he noticed roaches scuttling over the food.

When Sara Pichardo entered, wearing a white dress and a white cloth covering her hair, both garments bearing symbols similar to the ones on the walls and floor, she nodded to Dempsey and indicated that he and Marina should take a seat near the table. The old man shuffled over, carrying a cup of tea, which he offered to Dempsey. After a brief excursion into paranoia he accepted the cup. Tepid peonia tea. The old man made a hurry-up gesture, encouraging him to drink; he gave a satisfied grunt when Dempsey drained every drop. Within minutes he felt an undercurrent of resignation growing in him. Not gloom, not a daunted feeling. A simple recognition that the situation was beyond his control and he might as well put aside his fears. The bright Spanish chatter, the drummers nervously fingering their drums, the frowning god on his flower-laden float, Sara Pichardo moving about, greeting her parishioners, looking in her white be-symbolled dress like she was made of the same stuff as the place she presided over—these things seemed to be folding around Dempsey, absorbing him into their body, and he began to feel easy with them, as he might become accustomed to the water of a hot bath. He recalled Paoli's mention of a massive dose of peonia and assumed that the tea had manufactured this feeling. The statue of Olokun caught his attention. He pictured it hundreds of feet high, towering above a city of flowers, and imagined himself wandering petal-roofed streets, stopping at a dark café with brass jugs hung from the ceiling, sitting at an ironwork table, feasting on chicken and rice. Sara Pichardo came to stand before him and asked if he was afraid. He smiled. Listen to me, she said. The words slithered off into a rapidly repeating echo. Listen to me listen to me listen to me...

"I'm listening," he said, and understood she was shaking him, her catlike face inches away.

"Through me you will join with Olukun," she said. "You'll vanish and when you reemerge, Olukun will be asleep in you. Steeping you in his strength. But it's your actions will win the victory, not his strength. You must be cautious. Do you understand?"

Dempsey heard drums. A pattering beginning to find a rhythm. A steady gentle rain in his head, interfering with thought. "Yeah," he said. "I understand."

"Your opponent understands more than you, but we will watch for you and help however we can."

"Help...yeah." Dempsey's tongue felt thick.

Sara Pichardo removed his patch and there was the floater, one flimsy strand with a bulge at its midpoint, gliding along with the smooth apparent slowness of a communications satellite seen from space, passing in a curving trajectory and vanishing into the corner of his eye, and the central mass hovering, amoebas clustered together for the purpose of group osmosis, their cilia aquiver. He felt a momentary fondness on seeing it, such as you might feel toward a scar that women like to touch.

"You have an advantage, too," Sara Pichardo went on. "You've seen how your opponent plays his tricks. You understand him."

Dempsey waited for the floater to rearrange itself into lines, a template, a precursor of what was to come; but it merely hovered, its outlines fluttering like the edges of a frying egg.

"He thinks he knows you, but he doesn't know what Olukun has seen in your heart. He'll be overconfident. Use this against him."

Sara Pichardo's expression was pure intensity, no evidence of worry or encouragement or of any emotion that might color the will. An unwavering animal stare. When she turned from him, the whirling of her patterned white skirt made it appear that she was being whirled up from the patterned white floor, taking shape and substance from it, like clay molded on a potter's wheel.

Marina touched Dempsey's chin, turned his face to hers. "How are you feeling?"

"Spaced. The tea fucking stoned me." It was hard to focus. Her features kept spreading, flying apart, and instead of getting the whole picture, he would wind up tracking a corner of her mouth, the pinwheel of an eye, the point of her chin.

"It's okay," she said. "You're okay."

"You promise?"

She ducked her head, maybe a nod, and let her forehead rest against his.

The rhythm of the drums grew increasingly urgent and Sara Pichardo paced about, giving her head a violent shake every once in a while, stopping to shout in Spanish as if engaging in an argument with herself, and Dempsey realized that the ceremony was on, that it had more-or-less arisen from the chatter, from all the social interactions in the room, in the same way her whirling skirt had seemed to rise from the floor, the way the drumming had arisen from her stare, and he thought how natural this was, life transforming itself into ritual, rather than entering the place of ritual through great doors and being locked inside the stone cathedral thought of god, as if god were so divorced by his majesty, you required a church the size of a spaceship to reach him.

A pot-bellied black man with a mustache and a receding hairline shot to his feet as if yanked by an invisible rope. Others followed suit. Dempsey's chair seemed alternately too small, too high, never just right. A sweat broke on his forehead and his chest constricted. The drummers were going off in crazy directions, steady elephant heartbeats, monkey rhythms, Chinese firecracker pops, and Dempsey found it difficult to concentrate. His head snapped to the side, a galvanic twitch; he saw the room in serial segments, things slotting into view, like a slide show. Heaped flowers; a patch of white ceiling; the corner of a chair; a brown-skinned Puerto Rican lady waddling in a half-crouch, pushing at the air with chubby fingers and sow-fat arms; Sara Pichardo naked to the waist and gleaming with sweat, cupping her breasts from beneath, thrusting them toward the self-satisfied little god on his flower-strewn table, lunging forward and then leaping away, as if to tempt and inflame. Sweat trickled into Dempsey's eyes. The structures of the floater were quivering like a web stepped on by too big a spider. He had gotten to his feet, he realized, and was wandering the room. The stooped black man had put on a bowler hat, lit a cigar, and was performing a rickety dance step. A drummer flailed at his drum skin with bloody fingers. A slender pale woman bumped into Dempsey and recoiled, her face a mask of fright. Marina? He spotted her again. Dancing, but not with her customary fluidity. Stalking about, snatching at the air, herky-jerky and spastic. This place, he thought. A fucking insane asylum. The nurses had cut off the lithium, the orderlies were dropping acid. He needed air, he decided. Cold air and quiet. He spun about, searching for a door. There was no door. Only white walls tattooed with squiggles and loops and ripply lines. A hot charge exploded at the base of his spine and his limbs spasmed. He staggered forward and fell, catching the edge of the table. Blearily, he watched a roach scurry away among the flowers, following a dark avenue inward. Dempsey wanted to go after it, to find his café, to sit with intelligent bugs who smoked brass water pipes and calmly analyze the unseemly pandemonium of the outer world. A second charge hit him. He sagged against the table, clung to it. The statue's mother-of-pearl eyes were swirling, leaking a pale mist that enfolded him. The drums settled into a unison rhythm, pounding, beating down the flicker of his thoughts, driving him deeper into the mist. Which was swirling, thickening. Something bad was about to happen. He could feel it gathering around him. A white cloud compressing, becoming small enough to fit inside his body. With a tremendous effort, he hauled himself erect. Then he pitched forward, his hands clutching at red flowers, scattering the plates. He made a feeble grab at the statue, believing it was the source of the electric thing that was killing him. His fingers brushed its base and then he was swallowed by a white darkness.

♓

A MEMORY OR A FLASH of visual freakery that passed for memory occurred to Dempsey as he stepped through the door of the storefront church, into the winter night. It was as if he had been separated from his body, made small, and was staring up at an aghast, sickly version of himself, sweat beads jeweling his brow, eyes bloodshot and glazed. If it was a memory, it seemed he felt a great deal better than a few moments before. Solid on his feet, no eye trouble. The drummers were pounding away inside the church and Dempsey decided that he could use some exercise. He glanced at the yellow cliffs of the projects and had an urge to explore, to confront, to bust some heads.

"Little walk on the wild side," he said to himself blithely, and unholstered his gun, checked the clip. "Little tour of dysfunction junction."

He started out strolling, but picked up the pace and before he hit the end of the block, he was power-walking, swinging his arms like the yuppie dorks he drove past on Riverside each morning on the way in to work. It felt good to be moving through the world again. To be testing himself. He passed in among the projects. The streetlights tracked him with shattered eyes. Muted gangsta chants and hip-hop beats trapped behind cracked windows stuffed with dirty blankets and patched with cardboard worked their rhythms into his stride. He came to a lighted alcove in which two men dressed in hooded coats sat beside a bank of mailboxes, the heavily tagged steps beneath their feet like a Mandarin sub-title translating their whispery speech.

"Hey, *puto!*" one said to Dempsey. "You want something?"

"Thanks for asking. I'd love some heroin," Dempsey said jauntily, breaking stride. "You guys holding?"

"Heroin?" They laughed, their faces surfacing partially from the shadows of their hoods. "Where you think you at, man?"

There was something inappropriate about the attitude this response reflected. Dempsey understood the challenge, but it seemed they were bemused by his asking about dope. "I'm right here," he told them. "Where do you think I am?"

The men conferred, whispering again, and one said, "Hey, you the man, ain'tcha?"

"You scrubs been watching too much old TV. Too much *Baretta* and shit. Nobody says 'the man' anymore."

"He don't know," one man said; the other, pushing up to his feet, said, "Naw, he knows, but he ain't working with it yet." He jammed his hands into his jacket pockets and looked to Dempsey. "Keep going a couple of blocks. You find what you need."

A crablike uneasiness settled between Dempsey's shoulderblades, but his sense of well-being wouldn't allow it to get comfortable. The street was unusually clean, he noticed. No flattened cans, smashed bottles, demolished appliances, frozen cat corpses. Nothing but asphalt, concrete, and snow… and the snow looked pristine in contrast to the usual city snow. A neighborhood eco-project, probably. High school kids competing for a trip to Disneyworld. He passed another lighted alcove. Two women were kissing on the steps, hands rubbing between each other's legs. They didn't give him a glance. Their lack of wariness struck him as odd, as did the open lesbian display, something that was generally viewed in a disreputable light in this part of gangland. But then, Dempsey thought, maybe he was behind the times.

At the third cross-street he saw to his left a brightly lit area a block farther along. People crowding the sidewalks, sitting on parked cars, hanging out despite the cold. Actually, it no longer seemed that cold. Brisk, but an undertone of warmth in the air, like early autumn. As he walked toward the lights he spotted an immense shadow slipping across a yellow facade, gliding over the building like a weird negative spotlight. He paused on the curb across from the lighted area. The shadow was identical to the tattoo on Marina's hip. Squiggly lines moving in conjunction with a squashed black oval as the image folded around the side of the building, slipping back and forth, up and down, exhibiting the aimlessness and quivering flexibility of cellular life. Like the floater, he realized. He drew his gun, held it down by his thigh, and wondered why he wasn't afraid. The black sun slithered higher on the building, sliding partway up onto the roof—Dempsey thought of a lizard sleeping atop a wall with its tail dangling off the edge. He scanned the crowd, searching for Pinero.

"Hey," he said to whoever might be listening. "Little help, okay? You said you're gonna help."

With a sudden display of energy, the black sun slipped down from the roof and took up a position dead center of the building. The oval looked darker than before and obscured about a third of the windows.

"Now would be good," Dempsey said.

As he crossed the street something shifted inside him—not an uneasy shifting, but smoothly reflexive, like a natural accommodation to some change in stress or applied force, and glancing up, he saw that the sky was streaked with fire. He recalled the place he'd visited during the rave: dirty yellow monoliths ringing an eyepatch-shaped absence and cometary passages overhead. This time it didn't trouble him overmuch to realize he was far from home; in fact, he was developing a fondness for the place, a feeling of attachment similar to that he had for the Beach.

The sidewalks teemed with a procession of street meat. Hookers; high-school-age bangers; Puerto Rican eighth-grade angels showing off their new tits; hawk-faced young guys with mustaches trimmed to a thin line, like insignia. Yet they were not altogether what he had expected. The vibe of wasted hopelessness that usually radiated from such a scene was missing. There was an energy here, an unaccountable atmosphere of raw ascendancy. It was apparent in the way people smiled, the way they stepped aside to let others pass. The hookers were conservatively dressed in jeans and tube tops, not aggressive in their solicitations, but casual as shopgirls waiting for a bus. The children chasing each other through the crowd were playing, not settling a playground debt. The shopkeepers did not look paranoid. The young men smoked, threw fake punches at their friends, eyed the girls who passed, but Dempsey saw no exchanges of money, no palmed cellophane packets, no gang sign. Despite the hip-hop soundtrack blasting from the storefronts, the Shakira poster in a music store window, contemporary ads and dress, it was another time, it was fifty-years-ago in modern drag. Dangerous and impoverished, but as yet uncorrupted by the sins of Vietnam and the *contras* and Panama and the rest of the national karmic debt. Dempsey pulled back from his observation of the place, reminding himself that he needed to take care of business. He studied the building on which the black sun hovered centrally. He should, he told himself, take a stroll around the block. Inspect the exits. That was the path of caution and Sara Pichardo had advised caution. But a certain amount of incaution might be called for in this case. Incaution in the service of caution. Felonious action in the interest of crime prevention. Take a page from Pinero's book. Pull down a fire escape on the dark side of the building and break into an apartment a few floors up. One that was occupied by somebody vulnerable. A mom with her kid, an old couple. Ask a few questions. Pinero lived for such moments.

"Billy?"

For a second he didn't spot who had called, then he saw Marina threading her way through the fringes of the crowd, stuffing something into her hip pocket. She was dressed like one of the hookers, in tight black jeans and a matching tube top. Her lips were drawn cruelly red, her eyes encaverned by mascara and dark green shadow. Before he could speak, she latched onto his arm and said, "This way!" and began hauling him along the street, past the black sun building, weaving in and out among the passers-by.

"Are you crazy?" She twisted sideways to avoid a group of men blocking the sidewalk. "You were supposed to meet me downtown!"

He said, "What?"

She made a pissed-off noise and walked faster, leading him toward a subway entrance and then down the stairs. The platform was empty except for a handful of tired-looking men and women in work clothes, probably coming off a swing shift. On the wall next to Dempsey was a peeling poster advertising the Knicks, showing action from a game, but he didn't recognize any of the players. Marina lit a cigarette—there were no No Smoking warnings in view—and paced along the edge of the platform. "We gonna deal with these fucking monsters," she said without looking at him, "you need to get serious."

"'Fucking monsters'? What're we talking about here?"

She glanced up in astonishment. Astonishment turned to disgust. "Asshole!" she said. "You take this as a joke and we might as well not bother."

With a violent clattering, a train passed in an adjoining tunnel, its vibration raising dust and a smell of heated oil.

"We'll go down to the edge of the Patch," Marina said decisively. "Now you've been seen, we need to..."

"I don't think anyone noticed me. A couple of guys on Hundred Sixty-fifth hassled me, but that's about it."

Marina glared at him. "You don't want my help, just keep this shit up! Okay?"

She stood with her back to him, right elbow cupped in her left hand, taking quick, angry hits off her cigarette. It was like, Dempsey thought, she was a character in a story different from yet contiguous with the one in which he played a cop and she a bartender/dancer, and now he seemed to have been dropped into

· 111 ·

her story. If this was the help he'd been promised, he hoped it would become less confusing. He started to ask what she had meant by the Patch, then decided it wasn't worth the hassle—he'd find out soon enough.

On the train that carried Dempsey and Marina downtown, the passengers chatted, laughed, bummed cigarettes. No avoidance of eye contact, no hostile body language, no passed-out drunks and sleeping homeless. Whenever someone new boarded the car, they were met with a civil acknowledgment. It was the *Twilight Zone*, Dempsey thought. Manhattan on Ecstasy. An even stranger thing: after passing mid-town the train went elevated—there was no such stretch of track on the route of any downtown train he knew of—and they headed into the West Village; gazing out the window, he saw the rooftops were gathered under a dense shadow that stretched across the breadth of the island. The Patch, he assumed. Smaller shadows shaped like miniature black suns separated from its edges and glided outward, dispersing like scouts through the city, traveling across the facades of the buildings. Maybe, he thought, their fathering darkness had the shape of an eye patch. That would be in keeping with the fucked-up imagery of the trip he was on. The consistency of that imagery disturbed him. He wondered if the tangled filaments in his eye might be translating what there was to see into images he could handle, the reality more bizarre than it appeared.

"Don't let it get to you," Marina told him. "Just take care of Tico. All that shit down there'll fade away."

"Where is Tico?"

That irritated her again, but before she could accuse him of being less than serious, he said, "There's things going on here you don't know about. Drop the attitude and answer my question."

"The garden down at the end of Lord Street." She leaned away from him, as if to get a better perspective. "What things don't I know about?"

"I don't want to confuse you. One of us being confused is enough. What's Tico's full name?"

"Tico's all I know."

"It's not Manny Pinero?"

"Never heard of him."

"Is he a cop...Tico?

Marina laughed derisively. "Right!"

"I take it that means he's not."

"Yeah, he's not a cop. Fuck is wrong with you?"

"Nothing's wrong."

"Oh, yeah? They said they were sending somebody who'd deal with Tico, but you don't seem to have a clue."

"Who's 'they'?"

She reached into her hip pocket and removed a photograph and held it out. "This is you, right? Billy Dempsey?"

In the photograph he was thinner, sporting a few day's growth of beard. "You don't know me?" he asked.

"I know you resemble this picture. I know you're supposed to deal with Tico."

"But you've never met me before?"

"I was thinking maybe we fucked or something, but I'm not sure. I fuck a lot of guys." Then, after an interval, she said: "Quit looking at me like that!"

"Like what?"

"Like I won't give you a cookie."

Out the window, atop a domed building, a rippling banner that bore the image of the black sun.

"I meant you look sad," Marina said when Dempsey remained silent.

"I'm not sad."

"Then quit looking like you are. It bothers me."

"Anything else I need to know...'bout what's going on?"

"You know this is New York, don'tcha? The human race? Planet Earth? Shit like that?"

"If you say so."

"Jesus, you're weird!"

"Tell me about what's supposed to happen in the garden."

A shrug. "Who knows what Tico's got in mind? We'll find out."

"You're going with me?"

"Yeah, me and Izzy. We're gonna watch your back. Didn't they tell you nothing?"

Dempsey resisted the impulse to ask again who "they" were. It didn't seem to matter. Instead he asked, "What qualifies you to watch my back? Fucking a lot of guys?"

"I'm qualified, all right. Worry about your own shit."

They eyed one another for a few beats, then Marina said, "We got some time. We could check into a room and relax each other."

"Are you serious?" Dempsey said. "I gotta go against Tico and I'm gonna spend the next whatever rolling around with you?"

"What else you gonna do? Write your will? Come on, it relaxes me. You want me relaxed. I work better, I get the edge off."

"I'm already relaxed," Dempsey said, and realized with some surprise that he was, indeed, quite relaxed, living in the moment, not obsessing about what was to come.

"Do I hafta kick your ass?"

Until that moment there had seemed no more than a physical similarity between his Marina and this one; but in the way she was posed, her arms folded beneath her breasts, her expression reproving, yet with a hint of injured feelings showing through, Dempsey recognized a correspondence between the two, the same mixture of toughness and vulnerability in one as informed the other. While his Marina wasn't as vulnerable as she seemed, neither was this new Marina as tough, as brazen, as she wanted him to believe. Except for their veneers, they might well be identical. He wondered: if he fucked her, would that qualify as cheating?

"Just take it easy," he told her. "I got too much on my mind."

She tried to stare him down. Dempsey fielded her stare and said, "Y'gotta be kidding. You really wanna have sex now?"

"It beats the hell outa worrying about shit."

"I like to worry. Worrying makes me sharp."

Marina made a frustrated noise, then shined a crooked grin his way. "Your loss, man. You don't know what you're missing."

"Betcha I do," he said.

H

A S THE TRAIN BEGAN ITS DESCENT from the elevated rail, Dempsey had a vision of a future that might come to pass, or else the illusion of the Patch dispersed and he saw the truth that lay behind it. The rooftops and the shadow upon them vanished and in its stead there materialized a featureless black dome. Enormous. Miles in diameter. A great push of blackness that looked to have bubbled up from the bottom of Manhattan with such suddenness and force, it had shouldered off the buildings that had rested atop it and strewn massive chunks of concrete—some displaying rows of windows and decorative stone work—across a plain that spread to every side, creating a ruinous terrain of hills and twisting paths. The black dome pulsed, shrinking and expanding like a plasma body, and then, scant seconds before the train dropped back underground, a white light blazed from it—its entire volume filled with light so that it came to resemble a glass sphere half-extruded from the earth. Suspended within the sphere, almost buried in its radiance, was a snarl of black lines and beads that must itself have been immense and had roughly the shape of a spindle stood on end and was shifting ever so slightly, movements that, Dempsey realized, corresponded to the shifting of the floater, its pattern constantly evolving, like a living model of the lesser pattern in his eye. He felt an almost impalpable tugging in his humor, as if the floater were responding to its gigantic twin. Either Marina had not seen it or else she was so inured to the sight she expressed no untoward reaction, glancing at him idly as the train lurched and shuddered downward. Shaken, he toyed with the idea of the place, this city that did not yet exist or existed merely as a potential, speculating whether it had a history or if it was merely a stage, a central platform to which, if the black sun proved dominant, a ready-made history would then attach, providing false memories to the people who lived there...and perhaps those memories would be no more a fabrication than his own, fashioned of the same unreal stuff. The stuff of the floater must underlie it all. The improbable structure in his eye that was a simulacrum of...what? A metaphysical transmitter of sorts? Even in light of what he'd been through, he still had difficulty accepting this explanation.

Lord Street, both a street and a subway stop of which Dempsey had never before heard, was lined with brownstones, rows of leafless saplings along the sidewalks, little bistros and chic restaurants, well-dressed pedestrians, people strolling. A normal Giuliani-esque evening in the West Village except for the black sun shadows skittering across the brownstones, beetlelike in their agility. It felt less yuppified than the West Village Dempsey knew, having the busy, intricate smell of an actual neighborhood and not the arid odor of investment property. This, as had the hopeful atmosphere of the neighborhood from which they had come, continued to nag at him. He recalled what Randy had said about the new aspect of Olukun being potentially more violent and erratic than the old. The New York City he was familiar with, even those portions of Manhattan that had been swept relatively clean of blue-collar crime, retained an air of unlovely dysfunction, of oppressiveness and weary defeat and grasping amorality, whereas here the soul of the place—at least as it communicated to Dempsey—possessed a soundness, a healthiness, that his New York did not. He had the feeling he wasn't getting the big picture, that something was wrong with the information he'd been given; yet even as he thought this he felt a renewal of his determination to kill Pinero, as if his doubts provoked a chemical reaction that assailed the very heart of doubt.

Walking along Lord Street into the Patch, lagging behind Marina, Dempsey began to feel less out of place, though in some ways the neighborhood was alien to his experience. The buildings were similar to those they had left behind—brownstones, upscale groceries, clubs, boutiques, and so on—but were less well-tended; the pedestrians they passed displayed hostile attitudes more in tune with Dempsey's New York. Some were afflicted with disturbing deformities. Misshapen ears, eyes too large, freakishly long faces. A man leaning on a wall outside a bar smiled at them— Dempsey could have sworn that he saw doubled rows of teeth. With its grotesque populace and spills of red and purple neon illuminating the sidewalk, like a corridor whose doors all admitted into the same hellish interior, with its posters that advertised products and events of which he had no knowledge, the street had a weird glamour and radiated a feeling that was a distortion of the hopeful atmosphere prevailing in the rest of the city. Hope was there, but hope tainted by a lustful, feverish quality. Most of the glances aimed their way were challenging or aggressively sexual; the rest were fearful. People slunk and scurried from their path. Just like home, Dempsey thought; though his New York didn't quite have so pathological a stink. Judging by what he'd seen thus far, he figured the Patch might register a couple of degrees higher on the scale of aberrance. Not enough to make a significant difference.

Ten blocks along Lord, Dempsey recognized that the deeper into the Patch they went, the more extreme were the deformities of the people they encountered. A dumpy woman carrying her groceries in a pull-along cart had a mouth that stretched nearly halfway around her head. The eyes of two pretty girls in satin jackets and jeans were oval blotches of reddened skin that rippled as they walked. A man emerging from a parked car sported on his brow a tattoo of dots and lines that flowed into a variety of alignments, as if expressing in cuneiform-like symbols the language of his thoughts. Those people who hurried past too quickly for Dempsey to register their particulars dragged curiously configured shadows that implied more bizarre malformations yet, and the buildings, too, displayed deformities. They leaned together at rustic angles, their doors were misshapen, and the neon lettering in their windows was unreadable, an iconography of loops and whorls. The marquee of a night club drooped into elaborate gilt flourishes above concave windows, and the music that issued from within was whining, arrhythmic, like the orchestration of an overwrought nervous system. All suggesting that at the end of Lord Street lay the source of a contagion that was gradually transforming the Village into a lurid fantasy, one that accorded so neatly with the fantasy Dempsey had entertained about a voodoo-dominated New York, he once again doubted reality and thought that what he had seen from the window of the train, the gigantic replica of the floater, might be a more literal representation of the way things were, and they were treading along a section of a snarl of black lines suspended in light, a magical structure in the eye of a god. In the back of his mind there were questions beginning with "why" and "how," but they seemed asked by someone else, a minor functionary of his personality. He dismissed them as valueless. It was not, at any rate, the bizarre design of the place that concerned him, but rather its air of vitality. That signaled the challenge would be strong, the test a dangerous one.

The last few blocks of Lord Street were almost deserted, most of the streetlights dead, many buildings in a condition of decay. They gave out into an area of unguessable dimensions enclosed within an ironwork fence. The garden, as Marina referred to it, had the aspect of an arboretum gone to seed, an organic labyrinth with asphalt paths winding away into it and vegetation that pushed through gaps in the fence, extending feathery arms and spiky blooms between the bars, as if intent on breaking free. Dempsey was unfamiliar with most of the plants, but the largest of them appeared to be perversions of oaks and palms and maples. The oaks had grayish white trunks and branches that gleamed with a crepuscular insistence in the gloom, and the palm fronds were thin and reedy, like hairy feelers. From the limbs of the maples depended bunches of swollen gray fruit. In among the trees he glimpsed rooftops, but not the sort you might expect. These were of rusted tin and thatch, like shanty roofs. Seeing the garden, he felt even more strongly that his previous intuition had been correct, that this was an analog of the black dome he had seen from the train and the paths that wound through the arboretum were the tangled pathways of the floater. The place was not real, though he understood it was real enough to die in.

As they paused on the corner directly across from the garden, a diminutive black man wearing a green windbreaker and baggy chinos came out of the shadows of a nearby building and approached Marina. Dempsey, who was standing well away from Marina, his line of sight partly blocked, reached for his gun, but she began talking animatedly and the man responded with equal animation. She turned and said to Dempsey, "This is Izzy," stepping aside to enable the introduction. On seeing the man's cleverly made features, Dempsey felt that he had been heart-shot, slammed into by a hot penetrating force.

Izzy was short for Israel.

Israel Lara.

"This is Billy Dempsey," Marina said. "He's gonna take care of Tico."

"A real pleasure," Lara said, offering his hand.

Dempsey recoiled out of handshake range and slashed the air with a chopping wave that was as much defensive gesture as greeting. His mind twisted, trying to spin away from what it saw. The whites of Lara's eyes were as bright as they had been in the hallway almost a year before.

"Do you feel unwell?" Lara's gaze expressed concern. Dempsey could detect in it no hint of dissembling. He took another step back, his heart slamming. "I'm cool...I'm okay."

Lara continued to peer at him. "If you're sure..."

"Yeah...yeah. I'm fine."

The urge to run, to flee this ghost, this dread shape, was huge in Dempsey, but his feet were rooted to the spot as if under someone else's control. He tried to find reason for doubt, to pick out an element of the man's appearance that rang false, but the slightly receding hairline, the deeply cut smile lines, the pouchy cheeks, the single gold tooth...it was Lara. Another Lara, he told himself. This place's Lara. Not the man he had helped to kill.

Maybe.

What if his original instincts had been correct? What if this whole thing with the black sun, Sara Pichardo, and Marina was part of a complicated revenge scheme? First Haley dead, now he and Pinero drawn into an idiot duel. All orchestrated by Lara's spirit. Paranoia lit up his nerve ends. He had an acute awareness of a shadow standing in an alcove back down the block, of a sweetish chemical smell that briefly dominated the traffic fumes, of a streetlight shedding a dim, flickering glow, as if it were being smothered by the blackness in which it shone. The floater shifted in his eye like a snarl of fishing line adrift on an unquiet pond. "Who the fuck are you people?" Dempsey asked.

Marina shot him an aggrieved look and Lara said with some perplexity, "We're here to help you."

"Yeah? Who sent you?"

"He's been doing like this since I found him," Marina said to Lara.

"The church," said Lara, still perplexed.

"Lukumi Babalu Aye?" Dempsey was unable to look away from him, remembering the blood oozing from a hole in his shirt just below the collarbone, the darker bubbling of his chest wounds.

Lara made a dubious gesture. "Is this the name of your temple?"

Dempsey said, "Uh-huh...yeah," and had a thought that the *santeria* people must somehow be working the problem from both New Yorks, here operating like some sort of resistance, and maybe Lara was one of them. Maybe that was it.

"You seem to be having difficulty carrying the god," Lara said.

"Doesn't everybody?" Dempsey gave a shaky laugh, struggling to order himself, to still his fears. Ghosts. It was ridiculous. No more ridiculous than voodoo, but in terms of what had been going on, it was logical to believe that Lara was no ghost, that he was some other type of unreal creature. And what would that be? A snark? A boojum? A fell Tolkien character? Dempsey felt it all starting to get away from him, his thoughts sputtering into incoherence, spikes of terror sending cold signals down his backbone, into his groin. He seized onto a thought, clung to it as if it were a life preserver, tried to frame a question that would provide Lara with an opportunity of stating his flesh-and-blood credentials, and was close to succeeding in this when Lara stepped close and—before Dempsey could react—laid a hand on his shoulder and said, "Olukun."

The name stirred a little something inside Dempsey, generating a soft heat, as if someone sleeping next to him had shifted closer. The heat spread through him, evaporating paranoia, restoring a sense of calm equilibrium, and though he remained anxious about Lara, the issue was no longer paramount. The idea that Lara had more-or-less adjusted him, given his dials a spin, that was disconcerting, but he was relieved that his focus had been restored. He caught a rush, a burst of hot determination and valiant pride that flared up with such fierceness, it incinerated thought. He could barely feel his body, or rather he could feel only its heat, the chemicals of urgency and rage mounting in him.

Lara and Marina began talking and Dempsey prowled along the curb. He felt drawn to the garden. Compelled by it. Pinero was waiting out in that gray-green tangle, fat with confidence, his soul reeking of cordite, hanging loose, prepared for an easy kill. Picturing how Pinero would look, like he had before entering Lara's building, his pitted cheeks sucked in, tense yet fueled by a sort of oily delight, Dempsey felt his anger molding into a brutal shape. If Pinero assumed that he, Dempsey, would be rattled... It wasn't going to happen. All the lessons Dempsey had learned, the ones Pinero had taught him, they were going to jump up and bite the bastard's head off. The grimness of his anger suddenly seemed unnatural, nothing like his customary flare-ups. It was too formal and too steady an emotion, distinguished by an overbearing arrogance. Then he thought that given everything that had gone down over the past year, perhaps he had become a person to whom such a bleak attitude attached.

Marina and Lara broke off their conversation, and Lara asked Dempsey if he was ready. Dempsey was annoyed by his solicitude and chose not to respond.

"Once we enter the garden," Lara said, "there's a chance we may be attacked before you reach the village. If we become separated, don't worry. We'll know where you are."

Dempsey turned away from him, curious about the term, "the village," but not curious enough to inquire about it.

"That's right. We got your back, Billy," Marina said, a note of tenderness in her voice. "You just go for Tico."

Without offering an acknowledgment, his thoughts already gone ahead of him, Dempsey stepped off the curb and went at a resolute pace toward the ironwork gate and the violent opportunity that lay beyond.

)(

THERE WERE WHISPERS IN THE GARDEN and they were not made of wind, for no wind disturbed the leaves or lifted the branches. They had the sound of caught breaths and shuddery gasps, of invisible folk overheard in the throes of secret desire or fearful delight, causing Dempsey to imagine watchers at keyholes, vast identities whose normal voices would open the sky, but were attempting to be surreptitious, peeking in from beyond a barrier, curious to see how their brother in divinity might fare. An ashen gloom prevailed, and this false dusk seemed a byproduct of those ghostly exhalations, as did the sweetish vegetable perfumes that hung in the air. Walls of foliage bordered the path. Sword ferns and globular shrubs. Leaf clusters that looked too dark to be green charting the wend of serpentlike white branches. Dempsey carried his gun with its muzzle upward by his ear. Lara, holding a small leather sack in his right hand, and Marina, who appeared to be weaponless, followed at his rear. Except for those curious whispers, there was no sound, not even the faintest background noise, as if they had left the city far behind. After several minutes Dempsey realized that the path, though it was taking them farther from the gate, deeper into the tangle of the garden, was continually looping back on itself, a chaotic design that once again put him in mind of the floater, and he also realized the vegetation was becoming less dense. Through rents in the foliage he glimpsed dark shapes that looked to be human, but proved on closer inspection to be made of shadows and twisted tree trunks. On occasion he thought he detected a flutter of movement, yet he was unable to pin down the source. Nevertheless, he had a sense of watchful presence, a feeling manifest, not as a chill or gooseflesh or prickling hairs, but as a powerful excitation similar to that he had experienced when emerging from a tunnel onto a football field, the aggression of the crowd washing over him.

As they closed a loop in the path, Dempsey spotted a tree about twenty feet off the path whose likeness to a human being seemed other than coincidental. It appeared that the body of a young black woman had been magicked into a tree, her breasts and belly and legs merged with the trunk, her upraised arms evolving into branches, her drooping head swelling from the upper portion of the trunk like a large knot. The verisimilitude of the figure was undeniable, its features stated in sharp detail. Nipples, bellybutton, shaved pubic area. Full mouth and flared nostrils. Lidded eyes that snapped open as Dempsey came abreast of her. Pupil-less and blazing yellow. At his shoulder Lara made an angry noise and dipped his fingers into the leather sack. The woman began to separate herself from the cortex, her head lifting, hips writhing, arms lowering, tortured movements as if she were mired in mud, but growing easier, freer. The radiance of her eyes fanned onto her cheeks. Lara sprang toward her and flicked a whitish powder from his fingertips. Wherever the powder touched her, sprinkling over her torso, pinpricks of brilliant light developed, the same yellow as her eyes. She thrashed wildly about, mouth open in a silent scream, the leaves above her also thrashing, rustling, and as Dempsey watched, oddly unaffected by the sight, the pinpricks widened, gapping her skin, until she was scarcely more than a holed female fabric no longer able to contain the volume of light that had sustained her shape. Her figure collapsed and withered. The light faded rapidly and soon all that remained of her was ashlike scraps that floated down to settle in the grass.

From every side there came rustlings and stirrings. Lara stepped back onto the path, looking satisfied, calm, but Marina, who was now holding a knife with a curved blade, a purplish stain edging the cutting surface, shoved Dempsey forward along the path and said, "Keep going! We'll deal with this!"

A naked man with grayish skin and slumping shoulders and a sagging belly of such gross proportions, it hung down like a fleshy apron to hide his genitals, crashed through the brush onto the path and came lumbering toward them, eyes abrim with yellow fire. Marina pushed past Dempsey and, with a pirouette that reminded him of her dance at the rave, she passed close to the man, slashing at him. Light streamed from half-a-dozen rips in his skin and he began to dimple and shrivel. Other figures were breaking free from the prison of their vegetable forms, emerging from the tangled brush.

"Go!" Marina waved Dempsey away.

When he hesitated, she yelled at him and sliced open the chest of a gaunt, gray man who lurched onto the path beside them and made a swipe at Dempsey's head.

Leaving Lara and Marina to handle this business, Dempsey moved deeper into the garden. The sly whisperings returned and the twilight seemed to close down around him. Perched upon a branch overhanging the path, a grackle with eyes like nuggets of raw silver spoke his name, and shortly thereafter, a bulky, indefinite form off in the brush shadowed him for a while, crunching the undergrowth and emitting sepulchral growls, but never tried to close the distance between them. Dempsey sensed that the bird and the growler—like the tree people—posed no significant danger and had merely been deployed to unnerve him. He kept an eye out, but doubted anything would impede his progress. The challenge was to be decided between him and Pinero. It defied logic that someone allied with Pinero would want to kill him before he reached the site of the challenge. Yet the presence of these theatrical menaces bothered him. If things were as Sara Pichardo said, if he was carrying a god, why would they think he could be unnerved? Once again he was led to wonder if all was as it seemed, if he knew everything he needed to know.

Before long the vegetation thinned and through sprays of leaves he saw two rows of houses. Unpainted shanties with thatched roofs and plank walls the same shit brown color as the dirt; and, central of them, a pair of adjoining two-story buildings of whitewashed stone, roofed with tin. Between them lay a dirt street patchy with grass. The village Lara had mentioned. Though it must still have been night back in the city, the sky above the houses was a featureless gray and the place had an unlived-in vibe that put Dempsey in mind of the Academy shooting course, a street with wooden facades in whose windows and doorways targets painted to resemble perps and victims would pop up. Muggers with knives, masked gunmen, schoolgirls, and housewives toting sacks of groceries. He paused at the edge of the street. Fuck was he supposed to do, take a walk down the middle of it and let Pinero potshot him? The test was supposed to be equal, he reminded himself. If such were the case, at that very moment Pinero probably was approaching from the opposite direction.

What would Pinero do?, Dempsey asked himself. What would he expect Dempsey to do? He gave these questions a spin and concluded that Pinero would realize that they would anticipate each other's moves, so what was the point of strategizing? He'd trust his instincts, believing they were superior to Dempsey's.

When you're in the dark, as Pinero had said, don't worry about what you can't see, focus on what you feel. What Dempsey felt was the need to go methodically through the houses. Eventually Pinero would seek to manufacture a confrontation. He'd try to draw fire, get Dempsey to expose his position. Dempsey's best shot was to outwait and frustrate him. Lure him into taking too big a risk. That Pinero knew he'd do this was not a factor. They both were so familiar with each other's game, their only choice was to play to their own strengths.

The closest of the shanties was a one-room wreck, walls leaning inward, the mildewed thatch of the roof caved in, the boards loose and bowed as from years of heavy weather. Like the husk of an old gray spider whose legs had been eaten. On the side facing Dempsey was a window, three of its panes clouded with grime and one busted out. The grass surrounding it was unlittered. If this were an actual village there would be chicken bones scattered about, fruit rinds, an upside-down wheelbarrow beneath the window, pieces of a bicycle strewn in the dirt next to it, a kid's broken plastic toy. It was simply a backdrop for a violent act. Holding his gun in both hands, Dempsey eased along the fringe of the brush until he was about ten feet from the side wall of the shanty; then he crossed the open space and flattened against the wall beside the window. He flashed a glance through the broken pane and ducked back. Took a second peek, then a third, repeating the process until he gleaned a picture of the room. Crudely carpentered table and chair. Every surface furred with dust. Someone in the chair, his head down on the table. A desiccated arm extending from the remnants of a sleeve. Sprigs of dry hair sprouting from a scalp worn through in spots to the skull. The sour mustiness of a body dead a long time.

Dempsey slipped around to the back door, gave it a nudge. It swung creakily, but opened with relative ease. After making certain no one was hiding beneath the window through which he had peeked, he went inside. Brown air, a brown smell of death so thick, it plugged his nostrils. He peered through the cracked panes of the front window. The street was clear. He turned his attention to the dead man. Something moved in the mummified palm. A black beetle scuttled forth and froze near the table's edge. Something odd about it. Dempsey bent down to the beetle. It had seven legs, not six. Arranged asymmetrically. Like a little living black sun. A similar beetle perched on the dead man's tattered collar. He prodded the head with the gun barrel so he could get a look at the face. Half skull, half tattered skin. Grievous blunt trauma wounds on the brow and throat. The larynx crushed. He couldn't have absorbed such injuries and stayed seated. Someone had propped him up post-mortem. A card holder protruded from the man's shirt pocket. Dempsey started to finger it out. The instant his fingers brushed the shirt, just that brief touch transmitted a hot charge to his brain, a flash of mad electric presence that shorted him out and sent him stumbling away. His heart stuttered and as the juice of what he had felt drained out of him, it left behind trickles of the man's memory. A fight. The black rush of death and then life again, but not a joyful life. A mind imprisoned within a corpse, incapable of freeing itself, driven insane by the knowledge of the body's corruption. And by nightmares. Horrid fakes of life into which it was occasionally plunged. Little scenes that counterfeited reality and then turned into Clive Barker trips. Dempsey couldn't bring himself to make a second try for the card holder. He wanted to refute what he had experienced, but he wasn't willing to risk the chance that he might be wrong and feel that ragged voltage sparking through him again.

In each of the next three shanties Dempsey found a corpse dressed in time-bleached rags, and while he made no effort to touch them, he was convinced they were alive, in secret torment, alternately experiencing the dissolution of the body and dreams in which the joy of life was perverted into a horror movie, and that somewhere along the street stood an empty shanty waiting for the living, rotting corpse of either Pinero or himself, that this was the fate of riders who carried a defeated god. The force of this conviction made him want to run and run until he reached a door leading to a world of more reasonable fates. But the core of strength and confidence that seemed to underscore his every emotion, even the sharp bite of terror, kept him going forward.

Six shanties, six corpses. Seven-legged beetles everywhere. They scooted from pockets, shirt collars, eye sockets. But not a glimpse of Pinero. The gray sky oppressed Dempsey. It was, he thought, the gray of the pure indefinite, the unrealized, the color of the uncreate. The field they were going to fight upon was a stage erected in the midst of an ultimate absence, suspended and supported by a flimsy framework of ritual. That flimsiness, the accompanying notion that at any second he might fall through the illusion of earth into infinite gray, an endless fall... that was more unsettling than the prospect of death.

Fuck outwaiting Pinero, he decided.

It was time to shake things up.

Before he could talk himself out of it, Dempsey sprinted between two of the shanties and across the street. A shot, the flattened pop of an automatic. The round threw up dirt to his right; another ploughed a furrow at his heels and then he was safe, bellied up to a whitewashed wall, his breathing rapid but under control. He thought the shots had issued from the second story of the adjoining building, but Pinero had probably changed position by now—he fancied himself a master of guerrilla tactics. Hit-and-move was his style. He might be heading straight at Dempsey this very moment, and with this in mind, Dempsey eased toward the rear of the building. Had a peek around the corner. Saw the tangled edges of the garden and the rear wall of the building inset by a blue door.

No Pinero.

"Hey, Billy!"

Dempsey couldn't tell where Pinero's voice had come from. The window he had fired out of... or maybe from across the street?

"Bil-leeee! I'm waiting for ya!"

Dempsey made for the door and kicked it open. The room beyond was empty of furnishings, but a stairway led upward from the interior wall. He raced up the stairs and entered the first room off a corridor and had a look out the window. The street was clear.

"Might as well go for it, Billy!!" Pinero shouted. "Sooner or later, that's gotta be your play!"

The voice was coming from the adjoining building. Pinero hadn't moved. It struck Dempsey that they both were acting out of character, that his sprint was every bit as uncharacteristic as was Pinero's staying put. He tried to recall how he'd arrived at the decision to break cover. It seemed to have been a snap decision, a to-hell-with-it kind of move, and he wasn't certain whether to congratulate himself for having gone with his instincts or to worry about giving in to a foolish impulse.

"I swear to God, Billy! You such a fucking pussy!"

Dempsey resisted the impulse to respond.

"I been having to wipe your ass since Day One!" Pinero went on. "Teofilo's on West Ninety-Seventh—You remember! I coulda let you buy it there! Truth is, it crossed my mind! I asked myself, What good's this puke needs a diaper every time we go out? Guess I knew I'd find a use for ya!"

Secure now that he knew Pinero's position, Dempsey relaxed a bit. The whitewash was laced with a multiplicity of tiny cracks—they spread throughout the room, almost like a decorative pattern, as if the processes of weathering and age had been remarkably even in their effects. On the right-hand wall was a carefully sketched layout for a mural. Two buildings rendered in fine lines, further defined by gray shadings. Bigger than those in the village. Like apartment buildings. Four stories and a stoop. Uniting them, stretching across the gap between them, a web at whose center a black spider the size of his palm presided. As this was the first sign of occupancy that Dempsey had observed, he studied the sketch, thinking it might have a signal importance, but nothing jumped out at him.

Pinero had stopped shouting.

Dempsey checked the street again. Clear. When he turned back to the mural he saw the spider had shifted its position. A feeling of weakness stirred in his guts. Maybe his memory was flawed and the spider had not been central to the web; but even so, he was certain it had been nowhere near the brownstones and now it was an inch from the corner of one sketched wall. He approached the mural, stopping a body-length away. The spider was not a true spider, but the torso and head of a black man supported by eight spiderish legs. A head that had been squished into a peanut shape. It almost looked real. Dempsey came another step forward, squinting at it.

The spider twitched a foreleg.

Dempsey let out a squawk, staggered back. He trained his gun on the mural, but there was no further movement.

Nerves, he thought. Fuck.

Suddenly fatigued, he rubbed his forehead with the heel of his left hand, trying to restore alertness.

The spider's eyes blinked open.

Two blazing yellow pinprick lights stabbed toward Dempsey and in fearful reflex, he fired. The bullet chewed a gouge in the stone and the spider scuttled away, darting over the web that, Dempsey saw, had spread throughout the room, the pattern of its strands conforming to the network of cracks in the whitewash. He fired twice more and heard shots from the building next door. Pinero had fired along with him. The spider had taken refuge in a corner of the ceiling. Though Dempsey didn't want to take his eyes off the thing, he sneaked a look out the window.

Clear.

He glanced back to the spider.

The ceiling had gone black and lumpy, sagging like the underside of a hairy decaying mattress. For an instant he couldn't understand what he was seeing. Only when he looked straight up did he realize that the spider's body had grown immense, obscuring the whitewashed surface. Its malformed head was directly above him, the lamplike eyes burning, jaws open in a snarl, exposing discolored teeth, one gold incisor, and a fat glistening tongue humped behind the teeth like a slab of raw salmon. Electrified with fear, he threw himself to the floor and emptied his clip at the spider—it vanished, winking out with the suddenness of a switched-off TV.

His heart slamming, Dempsey tried to regain a viable perspective, to gather the tag-ends of impressions, separating them out from the distortions of fear. He wanted to file the spider away under the heading of Illusion, but then it might be possible to file this entire experience under that heading—the most important thing to understand was what, if anything, the illusion portended. Deformed though it had been, the face had borne some resemblance to Lara. That gold tooth... Dempsey was pretty sure Lara's gold tooth was in the same position, but if it had been Lara, what the hell could he make of that? It was simply a trick, he told himself. Part of the freakshow intended to unsettle him. He wasn't certain he believed this, but it worked for now.

Stick to certainties, he told himself.

He was fairly certain that while he'd been blasting away, he had heard Pinero firing, and he was damned certain he himself had hit the ceiling, yet it was unmarked, as if the bullets had lodged in the spider and when it vanished, they had vanished along with it.

Shit!

He sat up and patted down his pockets.

No spare clip. No bullets.

He was dead certain of that. Hopelessness swept over him. Fuck was he going to do now? Maybe Pinero was out of bullets, too. Not that he could count on it. But maybe Pinero had encountered his own spider or something like it.

Dempsey pushed up to his feet, walked over to the mural. The web and the spider were missing, but the brownstones remained. The fineness of the lines in the sketch made him think of the corridor that had displaced reality back in the men's room of the Hollywood Lounge, and of the whiteness that had, in turn, displaced it. He felt a crawl of paranoia and spun about, expecting to find Pinero in the door.

But like the spider, the door had vanished.

As had the opposite end of the room.

It had been replaced by a horizonless white mist, swirling and featureless. Seeing this, Dempsey, having experienced a surfeit of white transitions during the past few days, was reminded of where he was...where he suspected he was. Floating in the oceanic white humor of a god's eye, insubstantial as a fleck of protein and stationed on a spindly structure that had generated the structure floating in his own eye. He waited for the whiteness to envelop him and when it did not, when he recognized that he had one choice, go out the window, he realized that everything Sara Pichardo had told him at the church must have been a lie. This was not a contest that would be decided by his knowledge of Pinero or by Pinero's knowledge of him. They were being manipulated, forced into a confrontation. Ever since the Hollywood Lounge he'd been spinning, and then he'd met Marina. Fuck, yeah! Marina. She had boosted the spin, gotten him dizzy. The whole deal had been a set-up to push him and Pinero into conflict. Of course it was one hell of a set-up. Little matter of an alternate New York, Lara back from the dead, tree people...all that. Dempsey was incapable of believing that he had hallucinated the entire business and if he had not, it meant that even though they had been manipulated, the black sun thing was likely for real. Maybe because the god was sleeping inside him, not conscious as was the case with ordinary voodoo possession, he, his human element, had required manipulation in order to move him to this point. He heard the sound of that logic, the insane clunkiness of it, but clunky or not, insane or not, it fit the circumstance.

"Billy!"

Dempsey went to the window. Pinero was in the middle of the street, gazing up at him and grinning. He had on jeans and a black long-sleeved shirt with the tails out. His hands were empty.

"You waiting for something to give you a push?" Pinero asked. "'Cause something will, that's what's needed to get your ass out here. You should know that by now."

The sight of Pinero infuriated Dempsey, resurrecting the grim anger he had felt prior to his arrival at the village, but he resisted the urge to jump down into the street. "Show me your legs," he said.

Pinero hitched up the legs of his jeans, one after the other; then he did a slow turn, exposing his back to Dempsey, patting himself down. "Satisfied?"

"Take off your shirt."

"Jesus fuck!" Pinero unbuttoned his shirt, shrugged out of it. He had on a wifebeater undershirt. His pectorals wobbled, his belly hung over his belt, but his arms were thick and Dempsey knew that under the fat there was plenty of muscle.

"I ain't taking off my pants," Pinero said. "So if you're scared I'll shoot you with my dick, you gonna have to deal with it." He chuckled. "You look pissed off, man."

Dempsey eased through the window, hung by his hands for a split-second, then dropped to the street, landing in a crouch.

Pinero said, "Very nice. Nice athletic move. See what staying off the pills does for ya?" He interlaced his fingers, cracked his knuckles. "You not gonna ask no questions, man? I figured you'd be all full of questions."

Trying to read Pinero's pitted face, Dempsey thought he detected a flicker of uncertainty. An unfamiliar strain of hatred ran through him like a cold stream.

"Giving me that WWF stare, man..." said Pinero. "What, you think you're the fucking Rock? All I see's this skinny Irish fuck with a death wish."

Dempsey slipped out of his jacket, tossed it on the ground and shucked off his shoulder holster. He began walking a circle around Pinero, cutting the distance between them ever so slightly. He felt light on his feet, strong. A little fear, but only enough to inspire, to fuel his heart.

"This silent act," Pinero said. "It's very effective. Seriously. Very Master of the Martial Arts. You gonna make those bird noises when you start hooking...like your man Jet Li?" He made a cawing sound and laughed. "Nothing to say, huh? No last words."

"Why should I talk to you?"

"You might wanta know what's going on."

"I know what's going on."

"You just think you know."

"Maybe," Dempsey said, continuing to narrow his circle. "But the big picture really doesn't matter, does it? Not to you and me."

The whispering, which had faded to a susurrus, swelled in volume and Dempsey thought he could make out words, phrases, but in no language he understood. The voices were excited, though. He could tell that much.

"Hear that? Got us an audience." Pinero gestured at the gray sky. "Celebrities in the house. Agwe, Erzulie, Baron Samedi. Damballa la Flambeau. Azacca. Oshun. Ghede."

The relish with which he spoke the names of the gods—this told Dempsey that Marina's professor had been right about Pinero. He was a true believer. That surprised Dempsey. He had assumed Pinero was working an angle with the *santeria* people, but now he saw that Pinero was proud to be the champion of a god, that this was more than a matter of life and death for him, it was a great opportunity for service…and maybe that was all his angle, maybe he expected some spiritual benefit to accrue.

"You should appreciate where you are, man," Pinero said. "Savor your place in history. In the cosmic scheme. It's the last good thing's gonna happen for you."

"You didn't used to be such a chatterbox. You sound like some fruit on the Psychic Hotline. This voodoo shit's softening your brain."

"'This voodoo shit?'" Pinero shook his head ruefully. "You're in for a rude awakening, pally."

His circle drawn sufficiently tight, Dempsey planted his right foot and aimed a side kick at Pinero's jaw—it glanced off his brow. Pinero staggered, avoided a second kick and backed out of range. He pressed a palm to his forehead checking for blood, and said, "That shit's weak, man!"

Dempsey stepped forward, landed two jabs followed by a right that cracked Pinero solidly on the cheek; he danced away from Pinero's clumsy counter and circled again, watching for openings. Pinero was already breathing hard. He squinted at Dempsey, turning with him, peering between his upraised fists. Dempsey feinted with a right and when Pinero bought the feint, Dempsey did a sweep kick, striking him hard behind the left knee, buckling the leg. He should have backed off, danced some more, gradually wearing down the mountain, chipping away until the bigger man grew winded and careless from fatigue; but Pinero looked helpless on his knees, off-balance. Dempsey threw an ax kick, bringing his leg straight down toward Pinero's neck. But Pinero was ready for it. He grabbed the leg and twisted, sending Dempsey spinning to the ground. And then Pinero was on top of him, mauling him like a bear that had been fishing in a river of cheap cologne.

Head butts, clubbing punches, slamming elbows, thumbs probing for an eye—Pinero went at him with everything in the arsenal. His breath hampered by Pinero's weight, Dempsey kept calm. He succeeded in locking up Pinero's right arm and tried to worm into a better position, looking for the opportunity to sink in an arm bar. Then Pinero dropped an elbow directly on his collarbone and a bright pain starred Dempsey's shoulder. He couldn't afford to wait any longer. He let Pinero begin to straddle him, got him overbalanced, and heaved. Pinero flopped onto his side and Dempsey, bracing his feet against the big man's neck and chest, levered the right arm across his knees, then lay back and pulled down on it, putting immense pressure on the elbow, bending it backward, doing his level best to break it. Pinero screamed, flailed with his free arm. The move would have worked perfectly but for one thing—Dempsey's collarbone was fractured at the least. He could handle the pain, but strength was ebbing from his left arm and his grip was slipping. Giving up on the hold, he rolled to his feet and put some distance between him and Pinero. The pain spread across his shoulder. Fuck! He'd had the son-of-a-bitch.

Pinero sat up, cradling his injured elbow. "You gonna have to do better than that, asshole." Unable to use his right arm for support, he climbed awkwardly to his feet.

Maybe some strained ligaments, Dempsey told himself. Maybe they both had one fucked-up arm. All things being equal, he believed he could still take Pinero with kicks and right hands. He'd have to be very careful, though; he didn't like his chances if Pinero got him on the ground again.

Pinero moved toward him, his right arm dangling and left fist bunched. Dempsey let him get just beyond striking range and whirled aside, delivering a light right hand as he spun past and then retreating. Doggedly, Pinero came after him, winging heavy shots when he drew near, landing nothing. By the time this process had been repeated seven or eight times, Pinero's chest and brow were slick with sweat, his breath huffed. The whispers in the sky had grown agitated. They had, Dempsey thought, an air of disapproval—whoever was watching didn't care for the way things were going. Dempsey liked it fine. Five more minutes, tops, and Pinero would be wobbly from the exertion. Then he could start working on his legs, front kicks to the thighs, strikes to the knee joints, and once he'd taken Pinero's legs, it was game fucking over. Whatever fatigue Dempsey felt had been washed away by exhilaration and the adrenaline of victory. All he had to do was stay out of reach a little while longer...

A woman's voice shouted, "Billy! Watch out!"

He glanced behind him, saw Marina standing by the doorway of one of the white buildings. Before he could determine the nature of the danger she had warned against, Pinero was on him.

Apparently too worn out to drag Dempsey to the ground, Pinero hung on him one-armed, and Dempsey managed to break free, but was thrown off-balance. He reeled backward and went crashing through a rotten shanty door and fell against a table where a hollow-eyed corpse in rags was resting with its head down. The table collapsed beneath his weight and he landed on a wreckage of splintered boards. Seeming to float toward Dempsey, the corpse fell atop him.

He lay choking on the foul air, staring at the discolored skull that had rolled down his chest to lodge against his chin. Wormlike tatters of desiccated skin clung to the cheekbones; a black beetle perched in its nasal cavity. He felt revulsion, not fear. But as he knocked it away, the contact sent a charge of undiluted terror through him and it seemed fleetingly that he was on a city street. New York...a New York of fifty, sixty years ago, the cars bulbous vintage models, the fashions outmoded, the women wearing white gloves, demure dresses, the men all in hats, and overlying fear was a good-to-be-alive feeling, a buoyant feeling that belonged to the man whose nightmare Dempsey was channeling, and he, the man, glanced at his watch and saw a seven-legged beetle crawl from beneath his shirt cuff, a sight that paralyzed him with fright, and then a woman's voice behind him said, "Where you going, sweetie? You walked right past me," and he knew better than to turn around because she would not be there, or if she was, that could be much, much worse, because she was his torment, his demon, and yet he also knew he *was* going to turn, that somehow she'd make him turn... Stunned, still half-possessed by the dregs of the nightmare, Dempsey looked up from the floor just as Pinero kicked him in the side.

Denying the pain, Dempsey caught Pinero's leg and wrenched him off his feet, but Pinero wound up astride him and began to rain down punches with his left hand. Dempsey blocked most with his forearms, but took a blow to the temple that stunned him and another that felt as if it dented the top of his head, stunning him further. He grabbed Pinero around the neck and pulled him close to smother the punches. Unable to strike at Dempsey's head, Pinero switched his attack to the body, hammering shots to

Dempsey's ribs that sent flares of fierce agony through his midsection. He was going out—he felt an eerie instability, as if his mind were a liquid film spreading thinner and thinner, and walled off behind it was a ton of blackness ready to rush in and bury him. Spit sprayed from Pinero's mouth, his flushed, pudgy face mere inches away. Ugly as a bulldog. Dempsey tried a head butt, but couldn't get any leverage behind it. Redness edged his field of vision. Fragments of mind trash whirled up from the bottomland of thought. Part of a song lyric. Something his father had once said. A flash of Haley sitting at his desk. He struggled to maintain focus, but Pinero kept slamming his ribs and scraps of his life were spinning loose like shit backing up from a plugged drain. He felt an irresistible desire to surrender, to go spinning away himself... Then a powerful surge of heat and energy mounted in him. It boiled through his head like a storm cloud, bringing with it a flurry of emotions. Fury and despair, outrage at the idea of defeat. Towering emotions, Shakespearean bellows of frustration and dismay, and though Dempsey understood—as much as he understood anything—that they were not his own, that they belonged to the god he carried, the image they conjured was that of an old bum sprawled across a sewer grating turning in his sleep, allowing steam to billow up around him. His focus restored, he tried another head butt. Landed it with sufficient force to slow down Pinero's attack. Clinging to Pinero's neck with his weak left arm, he groped the floor for a weapon. His fingers brushed a splintered surface. A piece of wood. He fumbled for a grip, secured it, and as Pinero broke free of his grasp, rising to a sitting position, a gloating look imprinted on his features, Dempsey brought his right hand up in a swift arc and stabbed Pinero in the throat with a daggerlike section of the shattered table.

For an instant he didn't think it had penetrated enough to do damage, but then Pinero's eyes widened and he clutched at the piece of wood. Blood spurted over his fingers. In quick succession his face was claimed by expressions of hatred, determination, fear, and—lastly—a cartoonish gape that might have signified awe. He tried to speak and only managed a gurgle. Dempsey reached up and jammed the shard deeper. The blood jetted forth, an arterial spray like that from a shook-up bottle of pop with a thumb half-covering the mouth. Pinero's lips reddened, he clawed ineffectually at Dempsey and slumped backward, toppling out of sight. A soft mulching noise came from his throat and one of his legs convulsed, knocking against Dempsey's knee—Dempsey knew what that signified. He wanted to shove Pinero aside and get to his feet, but his strength was gone, the fulminant rage had subsided, and as if all the exhaustion and strain of the last days were flushing through him, he felt sleepy, enfeebled, capable of nothing more than lying there and staring up at the thatch. Ratty, graying palm thatch. Spines protruding downward, some devoid of leaf material, others frilled by a hairlike residue. The entire surface bellying inward. His ribs and shoulder hurt, but the pain seemed far away, as if his neck had stretched to some ridiculous length and his head was in a different zip code. Fuck it, he said to himself. It was okay to lie there. Where did he have to go, after all? He didn't even know where he was. In a shanty with a couple of corpses—that much he could count on. But where was the shanty? He couldn't handle thinking about that shit now, he was on the verge of passing out... and that was okay, too. His eyes traveled across the thatch in fits and starts, making little jumps interrupted by washes of darkness. It looked as vast and complicated as a country seen from an airplane. A desolate, uninviting country in the grip of a gray season. Gray hills and gray desponds. Gray was cool with him. He could relate to some good ol' gray. Like a winter day in the city. Like the emotional valence of Manhattan. Like a trip down the L.I.E. Like concrete rivers and industrial lofts. Like the thoughts of subway riders, robbed of tone and definition by the roar of the train and the pressure of hostile stares. Like the whispers coming from beyond the thatch, a disembodied hubbub, articulating a chaos of ghostly emotion. Gray was familiar, an old friend, a relief. He could take all the gray life threw at him...

Anything but white.

♓

WAKING THICK-HEADED and woozy, with his eyelids stuck together, thoughts ensnared by the memory of some fugitive, harrowing dream, then the first gray seepage of light, stumbling up to his feet and gazing blearily about, Dempsey realized that his vision was unimpaired. The floater was gone.

Fucking A!

He held his hand up to the eye, providing a field against which he could test the clarity of his sight. Nary a fleck or a flutter. He felt like celebrating, but the pain in his ribs and collarbone prevented him from being too exuberant. At least they didn't appear to be broken...though he could have sworn they had been. There was blood on his shirt. Lots of blood.

Pinero...

Dempsey looked for a body and saw that he was alone in a long concrete room, much larger than the room at Sara Pichardo's church, the ceiling unpainted, gray, and a colorful mural adorning the walls and floors. On the two end walls were representations of thick jungle-like foliage; depicted on the side walls were rows of shanties and two white buildings that adjoined one another. Like the village where Pinero and he had fought. The floor painted to resemble a dirt street with patches of grass here and there...except for an elongated oval area at the center that had been scrubbed clean. The place where he'd been lying. It was still damp. Recalling the damp area on the floor of the party room at the rave, he could guess what had been painted there.

The idea naturally arising from the mural—at least it naturally arose to Dempsey—was that he and Pinero had been duped, probably by friends and relatives of Israel Lara. That they had been lied to and drugged, then lured to a room prepared so as to support the lies they had been told, and there they were induced to kill one another in front of an audience. The whispers. Maybe they hadn't been whispering, maybe they'd been cheering, making bets, laughing at the two cops they had deceived, and he'd been so doped up, he heard all this as whispers. The tree people in the garden? Halloween costumes and masks. All the rest a product of suggestion. It had been a shuck, a total con job,

Still muddled, he tried to sort things out. If Sara Pichardo and her congregation had intended an act of vengeance, now, with Pinero dead, their vengeance was only half-complete. To make it complete, it followed that they would attempt to frame him for Pinero's murder. And that shouldn't be too difficult, since he had done the deed. He imagined a lawyer basing a defense on the story he would tell. No way he would skate. The prospect of a life sentence in Attica cleared the remaining cobwebs from his head. He needed to learn where he stood with the department. Gray light came through an open door at the end of the room. He checked his watch. Just after seven. The night shift would be winding down.

Dempsey's jacket was puddled by the wall beneath the image of the white buildings. His gun was nowhere to be seen. Figured. He dug his cell phone from the jacket pocket, wondered why they hadn't stolen it as well, and dialed the squad room. Terry Syzmanski caught the call and after identifying himself, Dempsey asked if Pinero was scheduled for the day shift.

"Naw, he's on vacation."

"Vacation?"

"Yeah, he said somepin' 'bout Vegas, I think. Didn't he tell ya?

Aw... that's right. You still on leave."

"So what's going on?"

Syzmanski grunted. "What's going on is I'm havin' a fuckin' heart attack with all this goddamn paperwork."

"Who else is on tonight?"

"Hey, Billy. No offense, but I got an hour for gettin' this shit done. I got no time to schmooze."

"Sure. No problem. Take it easy, Terry."

"Yeah, later."

No show of interest. No attempt to prolong the call or to ask his whereabouts. They didn't yet know Pinero was dead. He had a little time to try and protect himself...or to get the fuck out of Dodge.

Dempsey noticed that one section of the mural was shinier than the rest. He walked over to it. The paint was tacky. A freshly painted shanty. He let his eye roam along the rows of shanties. Did they add one every time they enacted the ritual? Could they be double-banging with him and Pinero, both avenging Lara and taking care of the black sun business? Ordinary logic wasn't applicable here. He supposed it might be possible that he and Pinero had been two places at once, fighting here and in that alternate New York...and Pinero had stayed behind. Sitting in the analog of that freshly painted shanty. Already beginning to decay, to acquire a crop of beetles. He supposed further that the gods might have been watching them in both New Yorks, here dressed in the bodies of tiny old men and fat ladies and half-naked priestesses, sacred riders mounted on their steeds. From what he could recall of the ceremony at the temple, a good many of the celebrants had appeared to be possessed. Doing the funky robot, the Shango cakewalk. He peered at the shanty window. The artist had glazed the glass with tempera dirt and scratches, and had implied a jumble of forms within, visible as faint highlighted shadows. Dempsey couldn't make them out, but looking at them made him uneasy.

As he turned from the mural, his foot nudged something. A piece of wood, its pointed end gluey with dark blood. After a while he picked it up. He remembered how it felt to his hand the first time he'd touched it. The surface was rough and not ideal for fingerprints, but to be on the safe side, he wiped the wood clean with his shirttail and set it back down. It made no sense that the murder weapon wouldn't be part of their frame. They might have photographic or video evidence, but in a murder trial, as Dempsey well knew, the prosecution liked to have its ducks in a row. Weapon. Motive. Eyewitness. He could hear a defense lawyer attacking such evidence, suggesting that it was either posed or counterfeited, and saying that even if reliable it did not firmly establish that Mr. Dempsey had killed his partner and friend of long-standing, a man with whom he had stood shoulder-to-shoulder against gunmen and drug dealers, the depredations of yellow journalism and the misdirected revilement of an entire city, reminding the jury that the eyewitnesses were a conspiracy of voodoo cultists, all holding a highly publicized grudge against the oft-persecuted, undeniably heroic defendant. Lara's friends had taken great pains to plan things. The murder weapon was crucial. Their lack of concern about it implied that their vengeance against Dempsey might take some form other than a trial.

He slipped into his jacket, zipped it high to cover the bloody shirt, and had a look outside. The dirty yellow monoliths of Fort Washington. About ten blocks from where he'd parked. He had believed that once he got through the night his troubles would be behind him and he could quit playing cop. Realizing that he could not quit, that he would have to do more to guarantee his safety, eroded the barrier that had shielded him from weariness. His ribs burned, his shoulder throbbed. But he needed answers and, ignoring the stares of men and women on their way to work, going quickly and with his head down to hide whatever blood had spattered his face, he went in search of them.

)(

THERE WERE NO ANSWERS to be had at either the Temple Lukumi Babalu Aye or the Ellegua Botanica. Both places were locked tight and no one responded to Dempsey's bell-ringing. That left Marina. She had much to answer for... especially for yelling during the fight. Disrupting his focus. Of course she had been possessed. Apparently possessed. Allegedly possessed. He remembered how she had danced back at the temple. Gawky and jerky. Empty of grace. Like a puppet under the control of an unskilled puppeteer. And maybe she'd had a reason, one he was unable to grasp. He was starting to accept the proposition that the fight in the village and the fight in the room where he waked had occurred simultaneously, that they were loops in a complex knot he had not yet managed to unravel, and as he drove toward the Manhattan Bridge, what he observed seemed to support that proposition, albeit in a way that initially confounded him. He had assumed that when he killed Pinero, nothing would change; but a change had come to the city. The neighborhoods through which he passed were livelier, friendlier, cleaner than they had been. They did not exhibit the innocence and passionate excitement of those neighborhoods that had flourished under the rule of the black sun. The difference was one of degree. Less peeling paint, fewer boarded shop windows. The weather had warmed. In the casual street exchanges and the conversations of pedestrians and the unwatchful poses of grocers standing by their doors while women pawed over displays of oranges and apples and papayas, Dempsey saw a spark of vitality.

It was as if the spirit of the place had been boosted a single notch, the sluggish stream of life marginally quickened. Though not a vast improvement, though it would probably achieve no great good, it was clear that something had been won, something more than the right to continue on as before, and he thought this modest reward might explain why Sara Pichardo and her flock had manipulated him. It might not have been about vengeance, after all. Even an ounce of good was worth dying for in a world where hope had been reduced to a marketing platform. He had believed that once. That was why he had joined the force. Now he was tempted to believe it again.

Crossing the bridge, then dropping down into the grind and blare of Flatbush Avenue, he began to feel more sympathetic toward Marina, to recognize the quandary she'd been in—having to take part in a process that endangered him and yet caring for him all the while. He had serious doubts about her. Why had he been left unconscious? Why had she shouted a warning during the fight? But he was willing to hear her answers. He had too much evidence that she cared about him to reject it out of hand. He switched on the radio. A gassed faux-Jamaican voice, probably some guy from East New York, was running down a list of concert dates, interjecting reggae-snob commentary on the bands. Dempsey turned him down to a mutter. He made a left onto Tillery, the intersection clotted as usual with honking trucks and cars, with the sound of squealing brakes, and was almost broadsided by a panel van whose driver, a young black guy, stuck his head out the window, made a disrespectful gesture toward the sky as if to suggest cosmic forces were responsible for the near-collision and said, "This motherfuckin' corner gon' kill all our asses, man!!" Dempsey waved and drove on. Three blocks along Tillery he caught a red light and sat listening to the long uninterrupted breath of traffic from the Brooklyn-Queens Expressway, the unmistakable aggressive blat of a Glas-Pak muffler closer to hand. A warm yeasty smell was farting up from somewhere, as if gigantic loaves of bread were being baked in caves beneath the city, mixing with keen diesel fumes, and on the corner a beautiful blond girl with eyes iced in blue liner, her breasts lent sweet definition by a clingy sweater, was gazing longingly off along the avenue, seeing there perhaps some perfect resolution to desire, while her boyfriend stared with the same longing through the bars caging a pawn shop window at the sporty shape of a red electric guitar, and on the opposite corner an elderly couple chose the moment to slow-dance a few steps as they waited for the light to change, and charmed by this slight measure of enchantment, Dempsey, the unsteady idle of his car's engine gently shaking him like a vibrating chair set on low, was able for the first time since he had waked to enjoy the fruits of victory, to accept that it had been a real victory with a real prize. Whatever happened to him, he had worked this small miracle, stolen a snippet of the black sun's fire, and it had been infused into the current flowing through the city. If he had to take the weight for Pinero... well, he'd face that when it came time and rely on lawyer games. It wasn't like Pinero had been loved in the department, and the lawyer could use the information about his miscreance and Dempsey's stress to concoct a defense of justification and mitigating circumstances.

By the time Dempsey parked his car in Green Point, around the corner from Marina's place, his mood was soaring. He bought coffee at a bodega, engaged in a brief conversation about the Knicks, their latest woes, with the owner, and then walked to her apartment building, one of a pair of four-story red brick twins set side-by-side, and buzzed her. No response. Where the fuck was everybody? Whooping it up at the post-fight party? Toasting Olukun at the Voodoo Lounge? Celebrity roasting the dead god? Wherever, sooner or later she'd have to come home. He sat on her stoop in the weak sunlight and drank his coffee, watching the corner boys at their stand, sprightlier than usual in their rough play, their hard laughter coming like shards of glass sprayed up from the background traffic noise. Pedestrians were strolling along the sidewalk, enjoying the day, some with rolled Sunday newspapers under their arms. The weather had turned almost springlike, the piled-up garbage in front of the building heated sufficiently to yield a thin reek, and the warmth cored Dempsey's bones, making him easy and sleepy. It felt good to be sitting there, with his worries put on hold, just taking things in. A mental snapshot of Pinero's gruesome death slipped into view, but he shunted it into a deal-with-this-later file and smiled at two Puerto Rican mommies who passed by on the sidewalk, pushing their babies in strollers. They smiled in return and said, "Buenas Dias," in unison, a double hit of brown sugar. Dempsey closed his eyes and heard sirens and music, laughter from the souvlaki joint down the block, smelled greasy lamb and onions and sauce, and thought that he was going to be a realist about Marina, look at her clinically and listen to what she had to say and if it didn't satisfy then he would walk away, but he wasn't going to be a hard-ass, he would really listen, and if her explanations were reasonable, if her attitude was genuine, he'd let her back in… slowly, cautiously, but willing at every step of the way to let her in deeper. He studied the pavement beneath the stoop, the pressed cigarette-butt-and-leaf trash caulking the cracks, and watched a man decked out in a golf cap and a shiny Giants sweatsuit opening up a taqueria across the street, rattling back the metal gate, inspecting a stack of packages inside the door, and a skinhead with a swastika tat on his neck, all jiggy and hooked into his headphones, came past, doing imitation snare-drum noises and making groove passes with his hands, grinning at a skinny uptown-looking haughty redhead in jeans and a car coat who was walking a dog like a white shaggy rat, her left hand gloved in a baggy, waiting for her best friend to expel its teensy poop so she could hurry on home and read the *Times* and do Pilates exercises to tighten her ass—surprisingly, she smiled back at the skinhead—and a slender black man in a green windbreaker and chinos sidled out from a pharmacy down from the taqueria, stretched his arms above his head like he was signaling a touchdown, then leaned against the wall, lit up a smoke, and

Dempsey, remembering how Lara had been dressed, went cold for a second, but decided against paranoia. What was he going to do, lose it whenever he saw a black guy wearing chinos and a green jacket? He tamped down the bulge of his anxiety and turned his eyes elsewhere, continuing to be troubled by a sense of unease. Time slowed. An overcast slid in from the Atlantic, pressing on the city with the gray insistence of a lowering steam iron. The subsequent decline in temperature made people walk faster. Dempsey grew impatient. What the hell could she be up to? He checked his watch.

A black beetle scuttled from beneath his shirt cuff and perched on his knuckles.

"Fuck!"

Afire with revulsion, Dempsey shook the thing off. It sailed to the edge of the stoop, then hustled back toward him. A little seven-legged scrap of blackness.

Cold fingers pinched Dempsey's guts and a dread shape began to accumulate in his head. He leaned down for a better look at the beetle, which had paused beside his hip, like an onyx brooch somebody had dropped. He counted the legs. Counted them twice.

Seven.

Hallucination. Dream. Bad drugs. He sorted through the various explanations, but only one of them fit and he thought he knew now why the world had changed, why the black sun's energy had blended with the less vigorous energy of his New York...if this was the world, if any of it was real.

The god and the proto-god had merged, neither one triumphant; the fight between him and Pinero had ended in a draw.

People were coming out of the shops along the street and every single one was staring toward the stoop where Dempsey sat. The guy in the Giants sweatsuit, the haughty redhead, the hip-hop Hitler with his headphones, the Puerto Rican mommies, and the black guy in the green jacket and chinos, oh yeah, he was there with his arms folded, nodding, a stance and a gesture that bespoke immense gratification—they had all returned to bear witness to this judgment, and Dempsey, possessed by a feeling of awful helplessness and sorrow, a feeling in which it seemed he was drowning, wanted to tell them it wasn't his fault, he hadn't meant to kill anyone, but he had no voice, his tongue was a slab of lifeless meat, he couldn't move it, couldn't open his mouth...

The door to the apartment building opened behind him and a woman's voice, Marina's voice, said, "Billy? Was that you buzzed earlier? I was asleep, I wasn't sure I heard it."

Oh god, god, this wasn't true, this was not how it was supposed to be, but he knew it was, knew that the jumble of forms the muralist had painted in the shanty window was him and Pinero sitting together at a table, their heads down in mutual and reflective decay, alone with their bloody wounds and their nightmares and their beetles.

"Billy? Are you just gonna give me the silent treatment?" A pause. "Will you let me explain? I don't know if you want to hear it, but I can explain."

Another seven-legged beetle crawled from beneath his trouser cuff and struck a pose on the tip of his shoe. Dempsey didn't bother to shake it off. He didn't know if he could shake it off. What if he couldn't move at all...even in a nightmare?

"Billy! Please...talk to me!"

He could probably move, he told himself, he bet he could at least move enough to turn his head.

"I can't come out, I'm not dressed!"

The second beetle crawled off his shoe and scooted onto the vertical face of the top step, appearing to slide along it like the shadows of the black sun he had seen sliding along the faces of the buildings, and he thought maybe that's all the buildings had been, steps leading to this step, and he wondered if there had ever been a black sun, if it was only an emblem of death and torment, or whether that was true and the battle with Olokun was also true...maybe with voodoo everything was true. I'm sorry, he said voicelessly to the world, to the people staring, I didn't mean it, I'm not a wrong guy, I was tricked, and if you let me tell you about it, you'll understand and maybe you can do something to help me... please! I'm so sorry!

"All right! It doesn't matter you won't talk! That's fine! But I *am* going to explain what happened!"

The strain in Marina's voice, the tearful undertone—it was perfect, the very tone she would adopt if she were ashamed by what she'd done and deeply concerned about how he felt, afraid of losing him, and that gave him hope, a little hope, that she wasn't part of this, and that the situation wasn't what it appeared, that the beetles were hallucinations, dreams, bad drugs...

"Won't you look at me even?"

...but what were the odds on that? He was bound to look, though. He had to find out for sure. It would be okay. No abyss, no monstrous shape. He'd simply turn his head and there she would be. Beautiful. Naked except for panties and a T-shirt. Hurt in her face. And he would stand and say something gruff, but she would hear that he wanted to forgive her, that he was open to explanation. And that would be that, they'd go upstairs, they'd talk, they'd make love, they'd begin again, and everything else would prove to have been the product of stress and terror.

"You came all the way over just to sit there and stone me? That's great... really great. Maybe what I did was wrong. Maybe I wasn't altogether truthful, but I had to be that way. I swear!" Her voice broke. "Whatever I did to you, I don't deserve this kind of treatment."

I don't deserve it, he said to whoever was listening, and started to repeat his litany of excuses—I didn't mean it, Pinero deceived me, I was caught up in the moment, I wasn't thinking clearly—but then he thought about what he had felt in the corridor outside of Lara's apartment and realized that he had always skated past that moment and now he could not recall that he had experienced the slightest doubt about firing at the dark inimical figure waving something at them, he had been charged up on adrenaline and danger and the Pinero philosophy of justice with a bang, he had been into it, totally fucking into it, even though a few moments before and a few minutes after he had not been into it at all. Was that enough to warrant such a punishment? It didn't seem enough. It seemed flimsy, an aberrant impulse, insufficient to convict anyone on a capital offense. This wasn't right. He was innocent by any rational standard. He was contrite, remorseful, and not an habitual offender like Pinero. He was the poster boy for leniency. No... wait, wait! Dempsey got a grip on his panic. Fuck all this. It was a dream. Or a psychotic break of monumental proportions. Like that movie about the schizo genius guy who lived in this incredibly intricate world he had imagined, believing it was real. In the end he couldn't escape from that world, but he had gotten along by denying it. By not letting it bother him. And that was Dempsey knew he had to do. He had to turn around and deny whatever was there, no matter how terrible. He had to confront it, tell it to fuck off. That was the first step to beating it. The hardest step. He geared himself up to turn, drew deep breaths. He couldn't move. The people along the street were laughing, pointing at him. What the hell was going on? As if thought could produce echoes, the phrase kept resounding in his head. What the hell is going on, the hell is going on, hell is going on... Turn, he told himself. Turn the fuck around. Do it quickly, do it now. Please, he thought, asking for nothing specific, asking instead for everything, addressing himself to the blank place in his mental sky through which prayers rose up like smoke into nowhere.

"You're going to make me do something extreme." Once again Marina struck the perfect tone, a teasing lilt that overrode but did not completely disguise the strain, as if she were putting on a brave show, determined to win back his heart. "You want the whole street to see me without any clothes on?" she asked, and then there was something new in her voice, barely a trace of it, a touch of contempt and menace. "You want me to hafta come down there and get you?"

Winner of the British Fantasy Award 2001 & 2002

With many of our early books now out of print, only the titles and states listed on the following pages are available — and in some cases, supplies are very low. Order now to avoid disappointment from:

PS PUBLISHING LLP
HAMILTON HOUSE
4 PARK AVENUE
HARROGATE
HG2 9BQ
ENGLAND

or via the website
http://www.pspublishing.co.uk
or by e-mailing
editor@pspublishing.co.uk

UK first class postage — add £2 for the first book and £1 for each additional book.
Airmail postage for the rest of the world — add £3 (US$5) for the first book and £2 (US$3) for each additional book.

PayPal and most major credit cards accepted.
Please make sterling cheques payable to PS Publishing;
make $US checks payable to Peter Crowther

STILL AVAILABLE

THE DARKEST PART OF THE WOODS

A novel by Ramsey Campbell — Introduction by Peter Straub

Slipcased hardcover — £55/$80   Trade hardcover — £35/$55

A YEAR IN THE LINEAR CITY

A novella by Paul Di Filippo — Introduction by Michael Bishop

Hardcover — £25/$40   Paperback — £8/$14

THE UGLIMEN

A short novel by Mark Morris — Introduction by Stephen Laws

Hardcover — £25/$40   Paperback — £8/$14

THE FAIRY FELLER'S MASTER STROKE

A novella by Mark Chadbourn — Introduction by Neil Gaiman

Hardcover — £25/$40   Paperback — £8/$14

V.A.O.

A novella by Geoff Ryman — Introduction by Gwyneth Jones

Hardcover — £25/$40   Paperback — £8/$14

KEEP OUT THE NIGHT

Edited and introduced by Stephen Jones, the first in the new *Not At Night* series, featuring stories from Sydney J. Bounds, Poppy Z. Brite, Ramsey Campbell, Hugh B. Cave, Basil Copper, Dennis Etchison, Neil Gaiman, Caitlin R. Kiernan, Tim Lebbon, Brian Lumley, Kim Newman and Michael Marshall Smith.

Trade hardcover — £45/$65

RIDING THE ROCK

A novella by Stephen Baxter — Introduction by Gregory Benford

Paperback — £8/$14

RAMSEY CAMPBELL, PROBABLY

Edited by S. T. Joshi and winner of the *Bram Stoker* and *International Horror Guild* Awards, a 140,000-word collection of articles and essays written over the past three decades by Ramsey Campbell.

Introduction by Douglas E. Winter

Slipcased hardcover — £65/$90   Trade paperback — £30/$45

WHITE BIZANGO
A novella by Stephen Gallagher — Introduction by Joe R. Lansdale
Hardcover — £25/$40   Paperback — £8/$14

JUPITER MAGNIFIED
A novella by Adam Roberts — Introduction by James Lovegrove
Hardcover — £25/$40   Paperback — £10/$16

LIGHT STEALER
A novella by James Barclay — Introduction by Stan Nicholls
Hardcover — £25/$40   Paperback — £10/$16

RIGHTEOUS BLOOD
A double novella by Cliff Burns — Introduction by Tim Lebbon
Hardcover — £25/$40   Paperback — £10/$16

IN SPRINGDALE TOWN
A novella by Robert Freeman Wexler — Introduction by Lucius Shepard
Hardcover — £25/$40   Paperback — £10/$16

INFINITY PLUS TWO
An anthology edited by Keith Brooke and Nick Gevers
Stories by Stephen Baxter, Terry Bisson, Eric Brown, Lisa Goldstein, Paul
McAuley, Ian McDonald, Vonda McIntyre, Michael Moorcock, Paul Park,
Adam Roberts, Lucius Shepard, Brian Stableford and Charles Stross
Introduction by John Clute
Hardcover — £45/$65

FUZZY DICE
A novel by Paul Di Filippo — Introduction by Rudy Rucker
Slipcased hardcover — £60/$90   Trade hardcover — £35/$50

BY MOONLIGHT ONLY
Edited and introduced by Stephen Jones, the second in the new *Not At Night*
series, featuring stories from Harlan Ellison, Hugh B. Cave, Christopher
Fowler, Tanith Lee, Joe R. Lansdale, Lisa Tuttle, Marc Laidlaw, Terry Lamsley,
Peter Straub and David Case.
Slipcased hardcover —£60/$90   Trade hardcover — £35/$50

TOLD BY THE DEAD

A collection of stories by Ramsey Campbell — Introduction by Poppy Z. Brite
Slipcased hardcover — £60/$90   Trade hardcover — £35/$50

JIGSAW MEN

A novella by Gary Greenwood — Introduction by Mark Chadbourn
Hardcover — £25/$40   Paperback — £10/$16

BIBLIOMANCY

Four novellas by Elizabeth Hand — Introduction by Lucius Shepard
Slipcased hardcover — £60/$90   Trade hardcover — £35/$50

DEAR ABBEY

A novella by Terry Bisson — Introduction by Brian W. Aldiss
Hardcover — £25/$40   Paperback — £10/$16   .

FLOATER

A short novel by Lucius Shepard — Introduction by Jeffrey Ford
Hardcover — £25/$40   Paperback — £10/$16

IN PREPARATION

THE HEALTHY DEAD

A novella by Steven Erikson — Introduction to be confirmed
Hardcover — £25/$40   Paperback — £10/$16

CHANGING OF FACES

A novella by Tim Lebbon — Introduction by Simon Clark
Hardcover — £25/$40   Paperback — £10/$16

LITTLE MACHINES

A collection of stories by Paul J. McAuley — Introduction by Greg Bear
Slipcased hardcover — £60/$90   Trade hardcover — £35/$50

GIG

Two short novels by James Lovegrove — Introductions by Eric Brown
Slipcased hardcover — £60/$90   Trade hardcover — £35/$50

TRUJILLO

A collection of stories by Lucius Shepard — Introduction by China Miéville
Slipcased hardcover — £60/$90   Trade hardcover — £35/$50

MY DEATH
A novella by Lisa Tuttle — Introduction to be confirmed
Hardcover — £25/$40   Paperback — £10/$16

THE PERIODIC TABLE OF SCIENCE FICTION
A collection of stories by Michael Swanwick — Introduction by Greg Bear
Slipcased hardcover — £60/$90   Trade hardcover — £35/$50

THE OVERNIGHT
A novel by Ramsey Campbell — Introduction to be confirmed
Slipcased hardcover — £60/$90   Trade hardcover — £35/$50

OUT OF HIS HEAD
A collection of stories by Stephen Gallagher — Introduction by Charles L. Grant
Slipcased hardcover — £60/$90   Trade hardcover — £35/$50

NOWHERE NEAR AN ANGEL
A novel by Mark Morris — Introduction by Stephen Gallagher
Slipcased hardcover — £60/$90   Trade hardcover — £35/$50

A REVERIE FOR MISTER RAY
A collection of essays by Michael Bishop — Introduction to be confirmed
Slipcased hardcover — £60/$90   Trade hardcover — £35/$50

FINE CUTS
A collection of stories by Dennis Etchison — Introduction to be confirmed
Slipcased hardcover — £60/$90   Trade hardcover — £35/$50

TURNS AND CHANCES
A novella by Juliet E. McKenna — Introduction to be confirmed
Hardcover — £25/$40   Paperback — £10/$16

BANQUET FOR THE DAMNED
A novel by Adam Nevill — Introduction by Ramsey Campbell
Slipcased hardcover — £60/$90   Trade hardcover — £35/$50

NO TRAVELLER RETURNS
A novella by Paul Park — Introduction by Elizabeth Hand
Hardcover — £25/$40   Paperback — £10/$16